YES

Other Phoenix Fiction titles from Chicago

Thomas Bernhard

YES

Translated from the German
by Ewald Osers

The University of Chicago Press

Published by arrangement with Quartet Books Limited.

The University of Chicago Press, Chicago 60637
Originally published in German as *Ja* by Suhrkamp Verlag,
Frankfurt am Main, copyright © by Suhrkamp Verlag 1978.
Translation copyright © by Ewald Osers 1991
Originally published 1991
University of Chicago Press edition 1992
Printed in the United States of America
16 15 14 13 12 11 10 09 08 07   7 6 5 4 3

ISBN-13: 978-0-226-04390-6 (paper)
ISBN-10: 0-226-04390-8 (paper)

Library of Congress Cataloging-in-Publication Data
Bernhard, Thomas.
    [Ja. English]
    Yes / Thomas Bernhard ; translated from the German by Ewald Osers.
  —University of Chicago Press ed.
     p.   cm.
    I. Title.
PT2662.E7J213   1992
833'.914—dc20   92-17921
                                              CIP

The Swiss and his *woman friend* had appeared at the real-estate agent Moritz's place at just the moment when, for the first time, I was trying not only to outline to him the symptoms of my emotional and mental sickness and eventually elucidate them as a science, but had come to Moritz's house, who in point of fact was then probably the person closest to me, in order quite suddenly and in the most ruthless manner to turn the inside of my, by then not just sickly but totally sickness-ridden, existence, which until then he had known just superficially and had not therefore been unduly irritated let alone alarmed by in any way, turn that inside of my existence out, and thus inevitably *alarmed and appalled* him by the very abrupt brutality of my undertaking, by the fact that, on that afternoon, I totally unveiled and revealed what, over the whole decade of my acquaintance and friendship with Moritz, I had kept hidden from him, indeed concealed from him throughout that period with mathematical ingeniousness, and kept continually (and pitilessly towards myself) covered from him, in order not to grant him, Moritz, even the slightest glimpse into my existence, which profoundly horrified him, but I had not allowed that horror to impede me in the least in my revealing mechanism which had, that afternoon and of course also under the influence of the weather, gone into action, and step by step, that afternoon, I had, as though I had no other choice, all of a sudden pounced upon Moritz from my mental ambush, unveiling *everything* relating to myself, *un*veiling everything that there was to unveil, *revealing* everything there was to *reveal*; throughout the incident I had been seated, as always, in the corner seat facing the two windows by the entrance to Moritz's office, to what I always called his box-file room, while Moritz himself, after all this was the end of October, sat facing me in his mouse-grey winter overcoat, possibly by then in a drunk state, which in the falling dusk I had been unable to determine; I had not, all that time, let my eyes leave him, it was as if that afternoon, after many weeks when I had not been to the Moritz house and had completely been on my own, which means reduced to my own head and to my own body, for a very long, though not yet nerve-wrecking, time in a state of utmost concentration *about everything*, resolved to do *anything* that promised me salvation, and finally, leaving my damp and cold and dark house and crossing the dense and sombre wood, pounced on Moritz as though on a life-saving sacrifice in order, as I had determined on my way to Moritz's house, to persist in my revelations and therefore downright improper hurts until I had reached a tolerable degree of relief, which meant until I had unveiled and revealed as much as possible of my existence which for many years I had concealed from him. At the climax of my, perhaps really totally improper, though desperate, head-and-body-relaxation attempt footsteps were suddenly heard in the Moritz house, footsteps totally unknown to me though not to Moritz who, needless to say, was also skilled in footstep-listening, and which Moritz had clearly been able to identify *instantly*, as I realized at once from Moritz's reaction to those sudden footsteps in the vestibule, since Moritz's acuteness of hearing was most extraordinary and of course, for his business, most convenient, and he, who until those footsteps in the Moritz vestibule had been sitting facing me, legs crossed, quite calmly and silently, if not indeed, as I suddenly realized, in expectation all that time, which suggested not just clients *interested* in property but *buyers* of property, instantly jumped up from his easy-chair and rushed to the door, in order to listen, and he had, as if not meant for me but more to himself, said *the Swiss couple*, whereupon suddenly all had become silent in the Moritz house; a moment later *the Swiss couple* had entered the office, the first people, apart from Moritz, with whom I had got into conversation for months, and with them, in the precise meaning of the word, the relief of my emotional and mental state, which I had expected and hoped for with the greatest urgency, though in fact forcibly and at all costs brought about by me that afternoon and prepared by me through my uninhibited revelations and, resulting from these revelations, my inevitable humiliations and shameless self-accusations *vis-à-vis* Moritz, had actually come about. At that very encounter with the Swiss and his woman friend I arranged with her, who of course was not Swiss but more likely a Jewess or Armenian, as I then thought, on no account a European, in the presence of the Swiss, who I instantly realized had no time for taking walks, to go for a walk in the larch-wood, and to this day I do not know how many walks I have had with her, but I walked with her every day, and often several times a day, and I certainly, at that time, walked with her more frequently and persistently than with any other person, and with no other person have I ever been able to talk about absolutely anything with a greater intensity and therefore readiness to comprehend, and therefore to think about absolutely anything with a greater intensity and readiness to comprehend, and no one has ever allowed me to look more deeply *into themselves* and I have never allowed anyone to look more deeply and more inconsiderately, and ever more inconsiderately and more deeply *into me*. While the Swiss was busy, in the small towns nearby, looking for door and window fittings, for bolts and grilles, screws and nails and for insulation material and marine paint for the concrete house which, as I learned from him at our first meeting, he had himself designed and which was already going up behind the cemetery, and in consequence was almost never to be found at the inn (the Swiss couple's quarters for the duration of construction), I myself, quite suddenly and probably at the life-saving moment snatched by the couple from my depressed state, or in truth from a by then life-threatening depression, suddenly found in the woman friend of the Swiss, who soon turned out to be a Persian born in Shiraz, an utterly regenerating person, that is an utterly regenerating walking and thinking and talking and philosophizing partner such as I had not had for years and would have least expected to find in a woman. Whereas she, the Persian, in the presence of the Swiss, with whom she had obviously lived for several decades, was almost continually, as though that had been a year-old habit if not a decade-old habit, silent, and not just taciturn as is very often the case in such a relationship, but almost continually silent, quite apart from the fact that I always remember her in an ancient black fur coat with a high collar she always wore turned up, from the moment of my encounter with her I had the impression that, like so many women in her position and of her age, she lived in permanent fear of catching cold, or indeed of continually freezing to death, that this woman would never be able to exist without that coat, without that fur coat which at one end reached down to her ankles and at the other had to cover and therefore to protect the topmost hair of her head, apart from the fact that, if she made any remark in the presence of the Swiss, she would contradict him, to my greatest surprise she displayed, in the absence of the Swiss, a need to talk, to be explained probably just by her stubborn silence *vis-à-vis* him or generally by her (presumably long-standing) oppositional attitude to him, not garrulousness but a need to talk such as may be observed time and again in all women who have lived for years with men like the Swiss, whenever their partners are absent, and so she talked. German was a foreign language to her but she mastered it, just as she did English and French and Greek, in the most agreeable and never really irritating way, and the very fact that the German she spoke as a foreigner, and moreover as a foreigner ultimately at home anywhere in the world and nowhere in the world, who had been born in Persia and had grown up in Moscow and attended universities in France, and who eventually with her one-time lover and present life companion, who, as she herself said, was *a highly qualified engineer and world-famous builder of power stations*, had travelled throughout the world, had produced in me not only a refreshment of my hearing and of my whole mental state, receptive as it was for such exotic speech melodies, by the manner of her speaking and thinking which, logically, gave rise to thought from speech and to speech from thought, as though the whole were a mathematical, a philosophical-mathematical and therefore consistently a philosophical-mathematical-musical process, she corrected and regulated and pointed and counterpointed my own thought and speech. For months I had no longer been used to converse with a person in a manner appropriate to my intellectual talents, in the long run I had inevitably become depressed by contact only with the natives, and even by my contact with Moritz, who undoubtedly, though not highly educated, had, for his circumstances, an above-average intelligence in every respect, for a long time I had no longer dared hope to meet a person with whom I might conduct an unlimited conversation, a person with whom I might enhance my conversational faculties, that is to say my thinking faculties; over the years that I have lived withdrawn in my house, concentrated exclusively on my work, on the completion of my scientific studies (on antibodies), I had almost completely lost contact with those people who, in the past, had provided me with confrontation, that is intellectual confrontation in conversation and discussion, from all those people I had, as I was penetrating more rigorously into my scientific work, progressively and, as I suddenly realized, most dangerously cut myself off and distanced myself, and from a certain moment onwards I had not even had the strength to resume all those intellectually necessary contacts, although I had suddenly realized that I could scarcely make any progress without those contacts, that without those contacts I would probably, in the foreseeable future, be unable to think, and soon even to exist, I had lacked the strength to arrest by my own intellectual *initiative* what I could see approaching me, the atrophy of my thinking, caused by wilfully incurred separation from all intellectual contacts and finally the abandonment of all contacts beyond the most indispensable, the so-called native ones, quite simply those going beyond the most urgent needs of existence in my house and its immediate surroundings, as it is many years now since I stopped corresponding, totally absorbed in my natural science I had missed the moment when it would still have been possible to resume discontinued contacts and correspondence, all my attempts along these lines had invariably foundered because, when all is said and done, I totally lacked perhaps not yet the strength but probably the will to do those things, and although I quite clearly realized that the road I had chosen and which I had followed for several years was not the right road, that it could only be a road into isolation, the isolation not only of my mind and thus of my thinking but actually the isolation of my whole being, of my existence which had always dreaded just that isolation, I had done nothing about it, I had continued along that road, though time and again appalled by the logic of that road, in permanent dread of that road but without being able to turn back on it; at a very early point I had foreseen disaster but had been unable to prevent it, and it had in effect occurred very much sooner than I had recognized it as such. On the one hand, the necessity to isolate oneself for the sake of one's scientific work is the prime necessity of an intellectual

9

person, but on the other there is the great danger that such an isolation is performed in far too radical a manner, in one which ultimately no longer, as intended, acts for the furtherance, but for the obstruction and indeed the destruction of that intellectual work, and from a certain moment onwards my isolation from the outside world for the sake of my scientific work (on antibodies) had had a destructive effect on that scientific work. That realization, however, as I was forced to realize in my mind in the most painful manner, invariably comes too late and what is left, if anything, is only hopelessness, that is the direct realization of the fact that the devastating, and therefore mind-and-emotion-devastating and finally also body-devastating state that has arisen can no longer be changed, cannot be changed by anything. The truth is that, before the Swiss couple put in an appearance, I had for months existed in my house in a state of *apathy*, in which, for a very long time, only self-observation had been possible and there could be no question of any work, let alone any scientific work, for months, admittedly, I had been waking up only for the most terrible self-observation, to exhaust myself totally in that terrible self-observation. I felt a continuous need to be with people, but I no longer had the strength for it and therefore no longer had any opportunity of making the slightest contact, and only by dint of a supreme effort of mind and body did I find it possible, at least at specific, quite simply existentially necessary, intervals, to visit Moritz, to spend a few hours at the Moritz home, which, however, was possible only with the greatest difficulties and invariably was an act of extreme self-denial. Intellectual people very quickly find themselves cut off from all contacts if they believe they have to concentrate on a scientific task or on any intellectual task generally; as far as I am concerned, I had believed that I had to give up all contacts altogether for the sake of my intellectual work, and step by step I had given them up, all of them, and I had offended a lot of people, and eventually everybody with whom I ever had any contact, by my decision to give up all those contacts, which, however, in view of my intellectual work, had always been a matter of indifference to me, my attitude with regard to my intellectual work had always been the most ruthless attitude, from a very early stage onwards I had never tolerated the slightest disturbance of my intellectual work, I had always, indeed all my life, swept out of my path anything that had opposed my intellectual work and therefore my progress with my scientific studies, and by doing so I had of course inevitably soon, through my own doing, found myself in isolation, and in the end I had been totally alone with my intellectual work and therefore with my scientific studies. And I had really believed that I could be alone with my scientific work, that I could bear, all my life, to be *only* with my scientific studies and that I could attain my goal with these scientific studies alone, but that was bound, gradually and then suddenly with the utmost certainty, to prove totally impracticable and totally impossible. Yes, I had truly believed that I could exist with my work alone, that is with nothing but my scientific work, without a single human being, I had believed that for a long time, a very long time, for years, possibly for decades, until the moment when I realized that no human being could exist without another human being or with his work alone. But as far as I was concerned, I had by then driven my existence much too far into isolation, so that there was no return from where I by then found myself. Thus, from a specific moment onwards, I was quite simply resigned to not being able to return any more. In that state I had existed in my house for many years and had made no more progress because I had given everything up. For years all my efforts to get out of that state had foundered at the first attempts. When I woke up I would wake up into total weariness of life. If I set anything in motion in the morning it was only ever the same mechanism of incapability of life and weariness of life, and there could be no thought of any, even the slightest, work, which merely aggravated my depression from one day to the next. Instead of being able to work I would sit for days, for weeks, for months, over my notes without being able to do anything at all with them. I would wake up and dread those notes and I would stride up and down in my house, first stride up and down upstairs, then again up and down downstairs, and I would increasingly relapse into totally useless activities which, inevitably, diverted me even more from my real work; what made me indulge in these pointless, in themselves totally pointless, activities and actions, was just as a diversion from my intellectual work, from my scientific studies and from the notes relating to them, which, as time progressed, I genuinely dreaded and which, by and by, I shifted to a room under the roof and there locked up so as not to come into contact with them again. The mere sight of those notes was giving me nausea. The mere thought of them. Years before, it seemed to me, I had come to a standstill in my scientific studies, the exact moment can no longer be established, I had missed that moment, had I not missed it I might perhaps have succeeded in realizing it fully and in analysing my whole condition, but try as I might, that moment and the whole processes at that moment have remained unclear to me to this day. It is possible, by realizing the crucial moment and by analysing everything connected with that crucial moment, to be saved. But I did not have that opportunity because I was not clear about the moment. My contactlessness, I realized, eventually proved my catastrophe, just as earlier on it had been a necessity and my good fortune; the isolation which I had prescribed for myself with regard to my scientific work and which, during the first few years of my occupation with natural science, had yielded me so many valuable results, and ultimately rendered possible for me the greatest conceivable advances, had now for a number of years been my greatest misfortune. However, realization without the ability to act had only made my situation more hopeless. The countless attempts at making contacts had failed at the outset. All those ideas for contacts had been stifled within me at their point of emergence. I did in fact write hundreds of letters to all kinds of people, in order to make contact again with those people, but I did not post any of those letters, all those letters had been addressed but not dispatched, stacked in the room where I had locked up the notes for my scientific studies. All these letters were addressed to friends, to acquaintances, to scientific persons, with a request for the resumption of contacts. I had written them, but even while writing them I had realized the impossibility of posting those letters, of dispatching them, of allowing them to arrive. Thus I had written letters for years without dispatching them, and deposited them in the room with my scientific studies. If solitude no longer had a meaning and if suddenly it had become unproductive, I kept thinking to myself, then it must stop, but I was unable to put an end to my solitude, to put a stop to my solitude. I had ceaselessly wished to make contact, but I no longer even had the strength to resume contact with my scientific work, so how could I hope to resume contact with human beings? This contactlessness had progressively developed into a mental sickness, the one I attempted to explain to Moritz that afternoon when I met the Swiss couple at his office. For years I had managed to conceal this sickness from Moritz, and yet, all of a sudden, I had to tell him about it, and that very afternoon when I made the acquaintance of the Swiss couple had probably been the climax of my sickness of contactlessness and simultaneously of redemption. I probably could not have gone on much longer in that state which paralysed almost everything within me, not another day, and I would, all the indications were present, have committed suicide, put an end to this existence, because revealing my sickness to Moritz alone and steadily talking at him would surely have been pointless and would inevitably have led quite simply to the deadening of my existence. The point was that the longer I kept talking at Moritz, whom I had ambushed with my self-accusations and revelations, the more pointless did these self-accusations and revelations I made to Moritz seem to me, what on earth made me bother that man, who was surely unable to understand me because he did not understand anything at all about me, with my revelations, that was what I thought while continuing ceaselessly and uninterruptedly to talk at that man, of whom I had all that time believed that he understood what I was saying, whereas in fact he had not understood the least bit of it, I should have known that to pounce on Moritz the way I pounced on him that afternoon was totally idiotic, that it was nonsensical, the very fact of revealing myself to Moritz and actually boundlessly unveiling myself to him, and expecting to be relieved and redeemed. As if intellectual hoards and intellectual rubbish had piled up within me over the years, I had, that afternoon, after crouching for hours on the floor at home, set out through the wood towards Moritz's house in order to discharge myself. I can still see the alarmed faces of his wife and his mother, as well as of his son, as I entered the Moritz vestibule, everything about me must have been *alarming*, immediately the Moritz woman let me go up to the office, where Moritz was poring over documents, a bottle of wine at his elbow, wearing his felt slippers. I had been unable to hide my excited state either from his family or from myself. I had immediately sat down in the corner seat, where I had always sat in the Moritz house, and staged my scene, by a sudden attack I had thrust Moritz into my terrible situation, I really never asked what he had done to deserve this, to have to listen to me. At that moment I only had that one person I could go to and I had always, whenever I was in distress at that time, exploited that person, as I did that afternoon. I just could not remain on my own any longer, must not remain on my own any longer, if I was not to keel over, if I was not to become dead myself. As a matter of fact, the Moritz house had so often been my only salvation that I cannot count the occasions, and that was how it was that afternoon. Today I am able to describe that state from some distance; a few weeks ago, or even a few days ago, I would not have been able to do that yet. Just as I have been unable to this day to describe that

17

encounter with the Swiss couple and especially with the Persian woman, but I realize that such a description has become necessary if I am really to perform an analysis of that time when I was near to keeling over. I had frequently told myself that I must not allow myself or permit myself to run to Moritz for relief every time I was dejected or in despair, but time and again I failed to stick to that resolution. The hospitality of the Moritz home had been the best, the nature of Frau Moritz, of Moritz's mother, the entire way in which the whole Moritz family lived, had been my refuge. I had always, even in the most hopeless situation, found shelter at the Moritz home. But I kept telling myself that I must not exploit the kindheartedness and the possibilities of that kindheartedness at the Moritz home beyond a certain limit, and sometimes I would control myself and would not go and see Moritz. On the afternoon in question, however, visiting the Moritz house had been inescapable, not having, as I mentioned above, set foot in it for several weeks, and the Moritzes probably had been all the more *alarmed* at my state on entering their house, because they had of course seen the state I was in. I was lucky enough to have been lost to myself, and I do not know now how I ever got through the wood to the Moritz house. I have overstepped the boundary of madness and even of insanity very often in my life, but that afternoon I believed that I had reached the point of no return. I had talked and talked and, by continually talking at him, misused Moritz in the vilest manner. Yet Moritz had submitted to all that, just as he very often submitted to vile verbal maltreatment from me because from the beginning he had not been without affection for me. By letting me talk he believed he was calming me down, he was familiar with that process. But on the afternoon in question all that was undoubtedly worse than ever. It was all different from other occasions and even after some hours I did not calm down. Instead of the usual calming down, that afternoon could only result in total madness, I thought. At that moment footsteps had been heard in the Moritz vestibule and the Swiss couple had entered and a moment later stepped into the office. If the Swiss couple had not at that moment entered the Moritz house and the office, I would probably have gone mad that afternoon. As it was, I had, from one moment to the next, been drawn into the instantly unleashed conversation between the Swiss couple and Moritz, which was exclusively concerned with the Swiss couple's purchase of a plot and with the concrete house already under construction on that plot, which the Swiss claimed was the last in a long string of houses in their lives. The Swiss had time and again talked to Moritz about the favourable opportunity of smuggling marine paint from Switzerland into Austria and about his ideas concerning thermal insulation in his future house and about how many bolts he was going to have fitted to the windows and the doors and why he had ordered steel shutters for the windows facing the forest and how he himself had constructed an automatic opener for his garage door. They, his woman friend and himself, had in vain travelled about Austria for two years, looking for a plot for their house, and only when they had given up their search had they, through an advertisement in the *Neue Zürcher Zeitung*, come across Moritz and now had the ideal plot. It was a mystery to me why Moritz, who had otherwise always as it were *initiated* me in his deals, had never made the slightest mention of the Swiss couple, especially as he might have assumed that such suddenly appearing foreigners would have been of interest to me, that is what I thought, because there was no doubt that Moritz had closed the building-plot deal with the Swiss couple months before my encounter with the Swiss couple, and it was even more incomprehensible to me that he had never mentioned the Swiss couple to me, considering the unusual nature of that deal, for Moritz had always talked to me especially about his unusual deals, always instantly *initiating* me into an unusual deal, and that the purchase of the plot by the Swiss couple was a particularly unusual deal was obvious, because the Swiss and his woman friend had purchased one of the lots behind the cemetery which had, for more than a decade, never found a buyer because it was in one of the most unfavourable situations that could be imagined and because, considering such an unfavourable situation, it had been sold by Moritz to the Swiss couple for an exceedingly high price; now that I had learned which plot it was the Swiss couple had bought I was reminded of the many, indeed the many hundred, attempts by Moritz to dispose of that plot, of the many clients, at all times of the year and of the day, he had led across the cemetery and through the wood to the plot, all to no avail. I now also remembered Moritz's repeated assertion that every plot was saleable, even the most impossible, and that indeed there was a buyer for everything and for every object on earth, and that it was always only a question of time until that buyer appeared. And the Swiss had appeared, probably in the early summer, and had purchased the plot and moreover declared that it was the ideal plot, the one for which they had searched for years. What the Swiss couple intended for their plot was clear, at least after I had made their acquaintance, they were settling where no one else had wanted or still wanted to settle, and the Swiss had a few times, whether jokingly or not, uttered the words *declining years*, I can still hear them, and I hear them clearly. He and his woman friend were tired of moving apartments and houses every few months, the time had come for him, the power-station builder, to settle at a definitive spot, and there was a good reason why this spot was here and nowhere else. They had both considered everything pertaining to that spot. Their lives, the Swiss said, had logically tended towards that spot. He had only to complete one more commission, a power station in Venezuela, and with the completion of that commission his professional career would be at an end. Two or three major trips to South America, he said, and then there would be peace. He was thinking of a vegetable garden round his house, neither too large nor too small, a deckchair in the sun, a dog to guard the house and a cat as a playmate for his woman friend. He had been forbidden by his doctor to eat meat because he was suffering from a sick stomach, he would eat vegetables, from his own garden, that was good for one's health. He praised the air at the plot which he had purchased from Moritz for a quite indecently high price (he was unaware of that) and every other moment assured Moritz, who was a born real-estate agent and therefore property dealer, of his sincere gratitude. He talked while the others were silent and, not in the least bothered by anything, painted his picture of the world on the wall of Moritz's box-file room, his naïvely honest Swiss picture. His woman friend meanwhile was watching him attentively with boredom and hatred in her eyes, the way, I felt sure, she had watched him for decades. In Moritz the Swiss had an ideal listener, who responded to everything the Swiss entertained him with and who, time and again, encouraged him to a new flight of story-telling. The Swiss couple, I learned, had been Moritz's guests on several occasions and had got into the habit of appearing at the Moritz home two or three times a week towards the evening, which made their stay in an area that was new to them easier; they were each time invited to dinner at the Moritz home, just as they were that evening, and the conversation which had begun in Moritz's office in the late afternoon was continued, from seven o'clock onwards, in the Moritzes' so-called dining room, and there too the Swiss had been the main speaker. I myself had restrained myself and adopted an absolute onlooker role, only now and then had Moritz addressed a question to me or invited me to answer some question the Swiss had addressed to him, whenever he assumed that I was able to do so, basically they were all of them questions connected with the construction of the Swiss's house, where and how he could best obtain building materials or track down this or that specialized craftsman, which I could readily answer because, on the strength of my own experience of building and of everything relating to building, I knew my way about fairly well and moreover was well acquainted, and largely also personally acquainted and familiar, with most craftsmen in the building trade. I know for myself how difficult it is to come to a new neighbourhood and wish to build a house, anyone not wanting to fail at the very outset of such an enterprise does indeed have to overcome superhuman difficulties, and in such a situation everything is in effect an obstacle and a person feels like giving up a hundred times a day. Apart from the fact that the scenery and the people, and therefore the whole of nature, is unfamiliar, they also display, towards a newcomer, an absolutely unfriendly, indeed basically hostile, attitude, and that unfriendliness and that hostility threaten to stifle anyone wishing to settle there. The Swiss was fairly unconcerned by that, and his woman friend, who, in contrast to him, the brutal partner, was the sensitive one, had nothing to say, at least as far as the construction of the house was concerned, as I very soon observed. She had been totally indifferent when the Swiss spread out the plan of his house on the table, where dinner had been served a little earlier, in order to discuss that plan with Moritz in every detail. It was my impression that the house drawn up on the plan of the Swiss looked like a power station, and subsequently, when I actually saw the building itself, it still seemed to me like a power station, it ran counter to all my ideas of a residential house and its effect, as could scarcely be expected differently, was anti-human, it was therefore anything but a home for anyone about to retire, instead it looked from the out-side like a concrete shell for some machine working inside, one that needed neither light nor air. The Swiss had evidently designed his home, which he kept calling his *final home*, exactly as he had the power stations he had built all over the world. Anyone studying the plan more carefully found himself faced with a vast number of rooms in which he would never and at no price wish to live, but the Swiss was convinced that he had designed the ideal home, whose costs, moreover, had exceeded all ideas of locally customary housing costs and which had induced Moritz to ask the Swiss how much exactly his house would cost, but the Swiss had not named a sum. Everything in and about

25

that house was to be solid, the best materials, the most excellent craftsmanship. It was obvious that such a house would cost a lot. By way of contrast, however, the Swiss was of downright repulsive meanness, and avarice had quite certainly been his most original quality. Such a person, moreover, is full of mistrust, and this had been his principal obstacle in connection with the building of his house, because – and that he had demonstrated most clearly as he tried to explain his plan spread out on the table, not without ceaselessly lurking for recognition and praise, which on the other hand was proof of his own lack of assurance with regard to the building – he mistrusted all the people he had engaged for the construction, all the craftsmen, all the labourers, and altogether all the helpers and helpers' helpers connected with the construction, and he could not restrain himself and had to say outright that it seemed to him as if the whole neighbourhood, to which he had come with the greatest confidence *in everything*, now deserved nothing but his greatest mistrust and suspicion, in which he was not wrong. Moritz admired what had been shown to him on the plan and thoroughly, though mostly incomprehensibly, elucidated by the Swiss, after all this was the most unusual thing that any client building a house had ever expounded to him, moreover a man as famous in expert circles as the Swiss, who even that afternoon, shortly after appearing in Moritz's box-file room with his woman friend, and, as I understood from what was said, not for the first time, had handed round those photographs which showed him with the persons who had commissioned the power stations he had built all over the world, and which operated and produced electricity there to this day, showing him shaking hands with the Queen of England and the President of the United States and with the Shah of Persia and with the King of Spain. The Swiss had greatly impressed Moritz mainly by his expert engineering terminology and his explanation of the terms, and had moreover promised Moritz to bring him, in the near future, buyers for his plots, most of them Swiss like himself, serious and financially sound persons. When the Swiss at last came to the end of his explanations regarding the building of his house and had made a few complimentary remarks about the furniture in Moritz's box-file room, not without draining his glass of beer, which had remained full during his explanations of the plan, he and his woman friend said goodbye to the Moritzes and to me and walked out and down to the vestibule, with Moritz seeing them downstairs and, at this opportunity, assuring them of every possible effort and support on his part. The Swiss could rely on him, Moritz, in every respect, Moritz said downstairs, I could hear him on the first floor, even right in the box-file room. The moment the Swiss had left and Moritz was back on his way from the vestibule upstairs to me, I thought that the woman friend of the Swiss had at once agreed to my suggestion that we might walk together in the larch-wood. With the fewest words possible I had arranged that we would go to the larch-wood the following day, just before five o'clock, I would collect her at the inn, I had said, the Swiss would be travelling somewhere at the time, and she should wear solid shoes for the walk in the larch-wood, and altogether dress more warmly than usual, because, what with our recent rains, it was cold and muddy in the larch-wood. I had the feeling of having made a welcome suggestion to her. A short while after the Swiss couple had left I too said goodbye to Moritz and walked home through the woods. After weeks of sleepless nights I would again be able to sleep, I had thought while walking home and that thought had not left me and that night I actually fell asleep. What a good thing, I thought again and again, and ever more intensively, that I had gone to see Moritz, until this single ever-recurrent thought had calmed me and I eventually, I really believe for the first time in weeks and certainly in a normal and useful manner, fell asleep and therefore was not even condemned to this thought of after weeks falling asleep once more. Naturally this did not mean that I did not wake up several times during the night in order to occupy myself with what had occurred the previous afternoon and the previous evening, my departure from the Moritz home and the confidences and revelations I had quite simply forced upon Moritz, which surely had been nothing but base affronts to his person and then, at the climax of all that madness and nonsense, the Swiss couple's totally sudden entry into the Moritz home, which had assuredly been expected for a very long time by Moritz as he *without a pause sat and listened* to me, actually *wordlessly and totally motionlessly listening to me without a pause*, even though he had not given me the slightest indication in that respect, he had known that the Swiss couple could turn up at any moment and put an end to my scene, which probably stretched him, or overstretched him, to the utmost limit of his receptivity, he had probably, while I was talking at him and pouncing on him with all my horrible, but to him totally indifferent, nonsense, been waiting all the time for the appearance of the Swiss couple, and the Swiss couple had indeed entered the Moritz house at precisely the right moment, at that moment I had not yet exceeded the limits of Moritz's receptivity for my forays, and most probably Moritz had allowed me to indulge my excitement on that dangerous afternoon, dangerous to everybody, only because he knew that the Swiss couple would come and put an end to the whole business, and thus, while I had not yet heard the slightest sound, he had heard the Swiss couple's footsteps at the door downstairs and had jumped to his feet when I had not yet heard anything, had made for the door and had listened at the door, and at that moment the Swiss couple had probably not even got inside the house and I can still see the relief on his face when he was certain that the Swiss couple had walked in, no doubt rescuers to him from a *dreadful* situation, conjured up by my improper and monstrous and inconsiderate and base behaviour, because I had undoubtedly expected too much of Moritz that afternoon, I had, while facing him, seen *on* him what I had done *inside* him, what I had wounded *in* him, and that this had been done in the most inexcusable manner. But with the arrival of the Swiss couple it had all come to an end and Moritz had been able to leave me and go down into the vestibule because he had to greet the Swiss couple and I feel sure that he had taken into consideration the fact that the Swiss couple meant a rescue not only for him but, in a very real way, for me, that the Swiss couple's entry into the Moritz home was my rescue. Although Moritz was a tough and shrewd businessman, one of the toughest and shrewdest I ever knew, he was also, and that very few people knew or indeed would have believed, a sensitive, delicately strung person, in whom the sensitive options were by no means crushed by his massive and, as it seemed to everyone who saw him, brutal or at least cold outward appearance, as a more or less insensitive body, but had, as I very often discovered, emerged, and the way Moritz had acted that afternoon and the subsequent evening confirms what I have said. After all, he, Moritz, could, at the latest at the climax of my excesses, or at the very latest at the Swiss couple's arrival at his house, have bowed me out of the house, but he had not done that, on the contrary, he had at once very skilfully included me in the conversation with the Swiss couple and had also immediately invited me to dine with him and with them, and it had finally been him who, as soon as the Swiss couple had entered the box-file room, had immediately steered the subject of the conversation in a direction that would free me of my nightmare, namely to the construction of the Swiss couple's house, and Moritz had succeeded in what he had intended to do, to take me out of myself by a skilful steering of the conversation, which meant manoeuvring me out of my hopelessness, which he had not succeeded in doing without the Swiss couple when he was alone with me in the afternoon and which he would not have succeeded in doing either in the evening which followed. How often had Moritz rescued me from a so-called nightmare, from deep despair, though probably he had never been aware of it himself, yet in recent years he had always, at ever shorter intervals, been the one to whom I owed my existence, this is no exaggeration and needs stating here. That afternoon I had for the first time talked openly about my state, admittedly without the preliminaries which would have been necessary and had straight away with a dreadful clarity and with the greatest excitement informed him of my sickness, of my mental and emotional sickness, which had been bound to alarm him, seeing that over those years I had never enlightened him with regard to that sickness, even though he, Moritz, had very often come to experience the effects of my sickness, time and again, and always in a different way, but this is not the place to quote examples, and Moritz had, time and again, seen that I was suffering from such a sickness even though I had never given him even the slightest hint of it, had said nothing about it, had always been silent about it, so he was never able to make much of it, and all of a sudden that afternoon I had attempted an analysis of my sickness, even though the attempt was bound to fail from the outset and in fact went awry. But how could I have thought even for a moment of giving Moritz an analysis of my sickness while I was so excited and when I knew that one cannot make an analysis in a state of excitement, least of all a self-analysis. Thus my attempt at an analysis was naturally confined to confused and wild outbursts and invectives and to a, probably totally confused, blurting out of unqualified sentences which were of no use at all to Moritz. But I had at last achieved what I had no longer believed in, an improvement in my condition, the fact that with the help of Moritz and the Swiss couple I had, that afternoon and evening, made myself tolerable again. But these notes are not intended to be about myself but about the woman friend of the Swiss, about whom I have again thought very often and very intensively during the past few days, and perhaps I shall succeed now, after a number of unsuccessful attempts along those lines, in putting these recollections down on paper. The reason why I have talked about myself for so long is of course that I made the acquaintance of the Swiss couple, that is the woman friend of the Swiss, that is the Persian woman, on that unfortunate day on which, as I have said, I had run to Moritz in the greatest excitement in order to save myself and on which I had in fact, as I have said, been saved, and not least by the Swiss couple of whom, of course, I do not believe that they had gone to see Moritz that afternoon for the sole purpose of saving me, which naturally does not mean that I have not very often thought that *in fact* the Swiss couple had, that afternoon, gone to see Moritz in order to save me, but not to believe so is just as absurd as to think so. Now, after this explanation, I can speak about the woman friend of the Swiss, that is about the Persian woman, and at least make an attempt to fix my recollection of her, even though this can only be done in a fragmentary and incomplete way and, like anything written, cannot be done in a complete or perfect manner, now that so many attempts in that direction, made by me lately, have time and again failed. But anything to be written has to be, time and again, begun from the start, and time and again attempted anew, until one day it succeeds at least approximately, if never quite satisfactorily. No matter how unpromising it is and no matter how terrible and hopeless, if we have a subject which time and again, and yet time and again, grips us with the utmost persistence and no longer leaves us alone, it should time and again be attempted. In the knowledge that nothing at all is certain and that nothing at all is perfect, we should, even with the greatest uncertainty and with the greatest doubts, begin and continue whatever we have determined to do. If we give up each time even before we have started, we eventually find ourselves in desperation, and finally and ultimately we no longer get out of that desperation and are lost. Just as we wake every day and have to begin and continue what we have determined to do, that is to continue existing, quite simply because we have to continue existing, so we must begin and continue such an enterprise as the fixation of a recollection of the woman friend of the Swiss, and not allow ourselves to be discouraged by the first, and probably continually obtruding, thought that we shall fail in our enterprise. After all, there is nothing but failure. If at least we have the will to fail we make progress, and in everything, in each and everything, we must at least have the will to fail unless we wish to perish at a very early stage, which of course cannot be the intention behind our existence. When I went to the inn to collect the woman friend of the Swiss, who was referred to by everyone in the village as *the Persian woman* and therefore, quite correctly, not as a Swiss woman, and whom I have referred to, and shall refer to, as *the Persian woman*, towards five, as I had arranged with her, she was of course not ready; that women, no matter what kind, are never ready at any definite agreed time is something I have known all my life, and this was the case also with the Persian woman; while I was sitting in the bar parlour downstairs and engaged with the innkeeper's wife in a conversation about old furniture, though presently more about the farm operated by her husband, which meant about *her* affairs, not without following the innkeeper's wife's invitation to drink a glass of beer, I reflected on the relationship between the Persian woman and her companion, though involved, off and on, in conversation with the innkeeper's wife and taking everything of that conversation in, I tried to visualize a more accurate picture of the relationship between the Swiss and his woman friend, which, however, did not get me far, virtually everything about and between the two was bound to remain unclear to me, and anyway I could not possibly have any idea about the two, seeing that I had only met them a few hours beforehand, in circumstances which cast little light on the two; time and again I tried to throw some light into the obscurity of their relationship, but in vain, nor did I make use of the opportunity of questioning the innkeeper's wife about the two, for that seemed to me improper, it would have been no less than the exploitation of an opportunity and probably, I thought, I would have learned a great deal from the innkeeper's wife, concerning the two, but surely not the truth, because the innkeeper's wife would only have reported something or other sensational about the two, which was not what I wanted to hear, innkeepers' wives as a rule engage only in shameless gossip about their guests, telling all kinds of untruths, I had been aware of that and therefore had refrained from questioning the innkeeper's wife about the Swiss couple, even though she was expecting me to question her about the two, much as she endeavoured to make the talk about her dealings, her secret dealings in chickens and pigs, because there was also a large pigsty and an even larger chicken coop attached to the inn, the main topic, her intention of telling me something about the Swiss couple and especially about the Persian woman had been transparent. These people, when they arrived, must have caused a real sensation to the innkeeper's wife because foreigners were a rarity in this neighbourhood, and Swiss or so-called marginal Europeans, such as the Persian woman, were an even greater rarity, the whole village had probably had this topic of conversation for weeks, possibly for months, while the Swiss couple was about, that is what I thought, because of my isolation I had not heard anything about the Swiss couple and therefore could not know anything, I need only, I thought, have had the will to listen around and I would have actually learned a lot, and, because I knew the so-called natives only too well, probably the most atrocious things. I eventually derived some pleasure from preventing the innkeeper's wife from telling me anything about the Persian woman, time and again she had tried, in the middle of her merely pretended conversation about her business, to make some remark about the Swiss couple and more particularly about the Persian woman, but I prevented her by more and more cunningly and more and more persistently talking about her business affairs, on the other hand she was pleased to hear what I thought about her pigs and chickens and about her feeding-stuff purchases and her visits to the market and her husband's visits to the market, because she had long discovered that my opinion, whether on old furniture or on agricultural produce, was exceedingly useful to her, that time and again, even when she had begun to doubt it, it had turned out to be useful and therefore exceedingly profitable, because as a matter of fact I know a lot about pigs and chickens and about agriculture generally, if only because I have an agricultural background and have been interested in agriculture to this day, if only marginally, but agriculture has always been a familiar subject to me and I have never lost interest in it, and I therefore could always have a good chat with the innkeeper's wife about agriculture and related matters, and she valued my opinion, though only in a roundabout way, and that day, too, she had been curious to hear what I had to say, though on the other hand she had, that day, not been keen at all to talk to me about her agricultural business, which I had brought up, but only about the Swiss couple, the Persian woman, who, as I surmised, had had an afternoon rest and was still busy dressing; meanwhile it had become colder than the previous day, the rain was pouring down, and who knows, I thought, perhaps she would not go to the larch-wood with me, on the other hand I was hearing the kind of noises above the ceiling of the bar parlour, that is on the floor of her room, which suggested that the Persian woman was getting ready for just our arranged walk to the larch-wood. While I was drinking my beer and talking to the innkeeper's wife who, always in the same white blouse, grubby at the edges, was rushing this way and that across the bar parlour, I thought, as I had done before, how run-down this inn was, how neglected every-thing was at the only inn in the village, and a single glance through the open door into the kitchen was enough to dismiss any idea of ever coming to the inn for a meal. The Swiss couple of course had had no choice but to take up lodgings here, they had to be near their building site. While the Swiss had probably been about all day in his car, looking for ever new people and ever new materials for the construction of his house, his woman friend, I had thought, had enjoyed a rest, but was she altogether the type of person who went for walks, because I had invited her for a walk in the larch-wood without even knowing if she was a walking person, possibly she was a person who did not care for walking, even though she had time to walk, unlike her companion who had absolutely no time to walk, but how could I know whether the woman whose acquaintance I had only made a few hours before and whom therefore I did not know in the least cared about nature at all? While the innkeeper's wife tried to talk to me about pig prices at the last few weekly markets and continually expected answers from me, I was thinking of that, to me as yet totally unknown, person with whom I had arranged a walk to the larch-wood at a time that was the most favourable of all for such a walk to the larch-wood, meanwhile the rain had darkened everything outside the inn windows, but I had put a torch in my pocket, I was thinking, and I reached in my trouser pocket and produced the pocket torch and tried it out and it worked. It would have been wiser to drink tea rather than beer, I was thinking, while the innkeeper's wife, when I had drained my glass, came to the table to bring me a second glass of beer, which, however, I declined. She, the innkeeper's wife, wanted nothing in her life except to do business, she was born to do business and in her head there was room for business only and her entire being existed only for doing business, non-stop business, no matter what kind, and there was nothing else in her features. Everything about a person such as the innkeeper's wife is business. Intellect, emotions, all related to business. Business, never mind of what kind, is the only motor of their existence, business is the heart and lungs of such a type. But I was not repelled by the innkeeper's wife, on the contrary, just because she displayed consistency in my presence, indeed the utmost consistency, and moreover continually, without ever flagging in the intensity of her consistency, she attracted me. On the one hand I was repelled by her, on the other attracted. Her consistency attracted me, it attracted me every time I came into contact with her, but the *purpose* of her unremitting consistency repelled me. Simultaneously attracted and repelled by the innkeeper's wife I had actually always

41

enjoyed chatting to her, also because, more than anything else, I had needed a counterpoise to my work, to *my* consistency, though this was not, by a long chalk, such an unremitting and exclusive consistency as hers, I probably admired her consistency, even though its purpose repelled me, which ultimately was simply business and nothing but mere business. But the innkeeper's wife also had a very high degree of intelligence, an exceptionally high one for an innkeeper's wife. I had very often been nonplussed by her frankness. Above all, however, I admired her ability not, and indeed never, to slacken in her work, she did not permit herself the least respite, her willpower must always have been supreme, the kind found in people who had gone at an early age through a severe illness, one that incapacitated them for several and indeed many years, in her case a severe lung disease, exactly the same pulmonary disease which I myself had suffered from at the same age as she. Such people, if they are, in a manner of speaking, cured, are possessed by life as if by some truly dreadful existence and never come to rest at all, and live and exist all their lives and right through their existence in a state of excitement, in most instances in a state of supreme excitement, and with the greatest, the very greatest, willpower. Possibly and probably it was just that illness which I and the innkeeper's wife had gone through that had, probably, time and again bound us together with the greatest possible dislike and likewise with the greatest possible liking. Because just as I had always been repelled by the innkeeper's wife and simultaneously attracted, so she, the innkeeper's wife, had been simultaneously repelled and attracted by me. But this is not the place to describe the innkeeper's wife, what is interesting at this point is only how I managed that afternoon to compel her not to speak about the Swiss couple, even though she had all the time *wanted* to speak about the Swiss couple and especially about the Persian woman, and how I had succeeded, by ever new devices, in forcing her back into talking about her business, although she had wanted to speak about the Swiss couple, to report on the Swiss couple. By repeatedly, just at the crucial moment, stimulating her interest with regard to her business I had succeeded, again and again, in *not* enabling her to speak about the Swiss couple. This I had been able to gather all that time from the attitude of the innkeeper's wife: that for months now she had not been interested in anything more keenly than in the Swiss couple, and that she was only waiting for me to give her a signal upon which she could let go for or against the Swiss couple. Everything within her was waiting for that

43

signal. Initially I had wanted to discover as much as possible about the Swiss couple myself, but this seemed to me the better way. To question an innkeeper's wife about a person, no matter what person, would surely mean to let that person appear in a dirty light from the outset – that I did not wish to do. I could well imagine people's gossip about the Swiss couple, what these in every way dull and dull-witted people of the neighbourhood would have in readiness for the Swiss couple could only be repellent and vile. It is my experience that the natives are always suspicious of any stranger and that in their opinions, if they have any, they are dirty and vile, and the Swiss couple would of course be no exception. A stranger coming to the neighbourhood cannot be well-meaning and well-disposed and well-intentioned enough – he will be reviled and abused and, there are numerous instances, destroyed. Especially when this neighbourhood is the most backward imaginable. Two people who have lived together for years without being married and about whom there is nothing to be discovered except that they have money are enough for common character assassination. The people in this neighbourhood are the most inconsiderate, and for a stranger every one of them is a fatal mantrap if he strays into it. Of this the Swiss couple, as they had been in the neighbourhood for a number of months, must have an inkling by now. Indeed the Swiss had actually dropped hints in that direction at Moritz's, he already viewed the natives in a different light, capable of anything in every respect, certainly dangerous. But on the other hand, as I had noticed at Moritz's, the Swiss couple still retained an excessive innocence and did not as yet have all the necessary experience of the natives, else they would be bound to have reacted differently in many respects already. It was incomprehensible to me, and it is still incomprehensible to me to this day, how people who have knocked about all over the world and have therefore seen a lot of the world, can settle in this, anything but agreeable, neighbourhood, for whatever reason. There could of course be some intention behind it, some intention totally unknown to me, I had thought, and I had to control myself in order not to utter that thought aloud, because in that case I would certainly have received an answer from the innkeeper's wife immediately and would have had my own ideas about it, since the innkeeper's wife had certainly progressed further than I had in wondering what the Swiss couple were seeking or planning here, but I controlled myself and said nothing, even though I was unable to stop wondering what the Swiss couple's purpose was in building a house here. And there must have been some definite purpose behind the Swiss couple's decision to settle here. These speculations led to no result. Besides, I thought, it was much too early to speculate about it. First of all I would take my walk with the Persian woman. Just after I had warned the innkeeper's wife against acquiring more than six hundred pigs in the following year, because I assumed that, especially for such small pig-fattening enterprises as that of the innkeeper's wife, there would be a tremendous drop in pig-meat prices in the coming year, I heard the Persian woman above me walking up and down her room more quickly than before and then walk out to the passage and to the stairs. A moment later she was in the bar parlour, I had risen to my feet, and we had walked out of the inn. The innkeeper's wife had certainly looked at us *oddly* as we left. For my conversation with her it had been useful that I had just that morning read the so-called *Landwirtschaftszeitung*, the farmers' weekly to which I subscribe and which is delivered to me by the postman every Friday, as a result of which I am of course always extremely well informed on all agricultural matters; on the one hand I had the *Landwirtschaftszeitung* available, and on the other my own head, and in consequence I was always able to make some well-informed comment on agriculture and it had certainly been necessary to study the *Landwirtschaftszeitung* if I wanted to talk to the natives, who were all of them almost exclusively interested in agriculture, which was their livelihood, there was no conversation with them other than about agriculture if I disregard the fact that in addition they would talk about women and about strangers. This region is to this day, in our so-called highly industrialized age, almost exclusively an agricultural one and in absolutely everything rurally oriented, that is agriculturally. That had also been the decisive reason why I retired to this spot, at a time when I had suddenly and, even to myself, surprisingly become tired of ceaseless travelling, to one place or another, the condition of changing my place of sojourn every few days or weeks and of virtually never being anywhere for more than a few days or weeks, had become untenable, mainly because I had wanted to get ahead with my scientific work, my work requires a fixed abode, and through a coincidence, through the mediation of a friend with whom I had done business some twenty years before, I had made Moritz's acquaintance and Moritz had found my house for me just as now, ten or twelve years later, he had found a building plot for the Swiss couple, but it is obvious that I had paid Moritz a low price, an indecently low price, for my house, whereas the Swiss couple had paid a high price for their plot, in my case undoubtedly a very low price as against the Swiss couple's very high price, but then my house had not really been a house but a ruin, with not even doors or windows left, not even doorposts or window frames, and a native of course would have paid even less for that ruin but a native would not have bought that ruin, it took a townsman like myself to buy it and settle in it. My house in effect, when I bought it, had been nothing but a roof, full of holes and nearly all rotten, resting on crumbling though gigantic walls. But I was young enough to make the ruin habitable, I was determined to turn the ruin into a home within a year, with my own hands. I had as good as no money and I incurred as many debts as possible, without knowing how or when I would repay those debts, but the thought did not bother me, what mattered to me was that I had a place to myself in the world, one that could be enclosed and locked, one in which I could fully concentrate on my scientific work. No one can have any idea at all what it meant to make that ruin into a habitable waterproof building. But that is another story. What I wanted to say was that I chose this neighbourhood because, being in fact very backward and not yet touched at all by what is called progress, it gave me the opportunity of concentrating exclusively on myself, which means on my scientific work, which would not have been possible in any other neighbourhood which might otherwise, on the surface, have answered my ideas of a neighbourhood suitable for myself and which in fact has similarities, indeed the same structure, as the region from which I came, because the region to which I wanted to retire in order to get on with my science had to be similar to the region from which I came. The people, too, at the spot where, as I have said, I arrived by accident were like the people in my native region, just as hard and cold and, if need be, mean and despicable and merciless towards any intruder. But of course they did not exhaust themselves solely in their deadly and devilish peculiarities. Maybe the people in this region are even ruder than in my native one, maybe even colder, even more infamous. But it is a fact that a stranger coming to a, to him, totally unfamiliar region and among entirely new people, will always perceive them as much colder and more infamous than in fact they are. But my impression, and after all I have now lived in this neighbourhood for well over a decade, has not weakened in the meantime. I have to assume that every stranger coming here has the same impressions and reactions, so presumably the Swiss couple had the same impressions as me, possibly, being two of them, somewhat attenuated, though the Persian woman would certainly have had the same impressions as me, because we were like one another, unlike the Swiss who had a thick skin and a hard head. It was touching, the way she had dressed for our walk in the larch-wood. On her head she wore a man's hat and on her feet men's rubber boots, which, I thought, she must have borrowed from the innkeeper. Her fur coat was totally unsuitable for the rain, but she had wanted to take that walk at any cost. It was raining so hard I could not even look up and look at her, and the same the other way round, so we quite simply walked away from the inn and down to the larch-wood, for a while striding in silence through the sodden leaves, which made a strange sound which was pleasing to both of us, because we waded ever more deeply through ever more leaves, which we need not have done if we had kept to the path, but we disregarded the path. When two people who do not know each other, and who have seen one another only once before, take a walk together they first of all remain silent for a very long time, especially if they are a man and a woman. Which one will speak first is entirely open. In this case it was I who broke the silence by asking my companion where she had got the boots she had on her feet, and where she had got the hat she was wearing on her head, and I was immediately confirmed in my supposition, hat and boots belonged to the husband of the innkeeper's wife, I had felt sure in my supposition and I was once again amazed at my powers of observation, because I had in fact realized from the first that the rubber boots were the rubber boots of the innkeeper and the hat was the innkeeper's hat, I had established this from details about the hat and from details about the boots. Anyone living long enough and attentively in a region like ours and in a village like ours soon comes to know all objects and soon comes to know to whom all those objects belong, even, evidently, in the case of boots and hats, not to mention other, more conspicuous, objects. Of course I am trained in perception and observation in an especially thorough manner and therefore am possibly not a generally valid example. Such a gift of perception and observation is of the greatest advantage, but on the other hand also of the greatest disadvantage, and it is rarely welcome, almost invariably unwelcome. Such a person who perceives everything and who sees everything and who observes everything, moreover continually, is not popular, more often feared, and people have always guarded themselves against such a person, because such a person is a dangerous person and dangerous persons are not only feared but hated, and in that respect I have to describe myself as a hated person. Personally, of course, I regard my perceptivity and gift for observation as an exceedingly useful advantage, one which has often proved life-saving. Round her neck the Persian woman, apart from having the collar of her fur coat turned up, had also tied a woollen scarf, a very fine English woollen scarf which had probably cost a lot of money and which the Persian woman had no doubt bought in London, that was my assumption, which subsequently turned out to be correct. A few times, because the ground in the wood is sloping everywhere, she slipped and I caught her. But no conversation had got going, and after I had also asked where she got her woollen scarf, possibly an improper question as I had thought, I wondered if we had not better return. For a moment I had the idea of taking her along to my house, to show her my home, but then I dropped the idea: not to my house after the first walk with her, I had thought, and instead suggested to her that we should return to the inn and sit in the parlour and have some tea or, I thought, some cognac. Basically it was not she who barred a conversation or even any talk but myself, for I was no longer used to being with a so-called person of intellect and the Persian woman, as I instantly realized, was such a person of intellect, unlike her companion, the Swiss, who was no such thing. What had I expected of that walk? It ended with both of us, eventually her too, returning to the inn soaked to the skin and sitting down in the corner of the bar parlour. The innkeeper's wife had brought us two cognacs. But even in the bar parlour conversation had been out of the question, not even a chat had materialized because the innkeeper's wife had continuously been present, she had, in expectation of a conversation between me and the Persian woman, sat down with some knitting in the bar parlour and, so it seemed to me, settled down for good by the bar. There she sat and waited. But no conversation had got going between me and the Persian woman. But in point of fact there was no need whatever of an audible conversation because we had, for quite a while, even though not with uttered words, been conversing. We conversed silently and our conversation was one of the most stimulating imaginable; words uttered and strung together for the ears could not have had such an effect as that silence. Thus we sat in the bar parlour for more than an hour, wordlessly but in rather an agreeable state. The innkeeper's wife, to whom this behaviour must have seemed mysterious, had of course been disappointed. She had brought us two more cognacs, charged them to me, and had meanwhile placed the rubber boots next to the stove and hung up the hat to dry. She had also hung up the fur coat over the drying rods above the stove. It would have been interesting to know what went on inside her while she was knitting. Her demeanour and the way she now and again looked across at us contained a lot of questions and also the answers to them. A labourer who had suddenly entered the bar parlour, one of the beer hauliers resident in the village, who had sat down at the next table and ordered a beer, was destined to bring the scene to an end. The innkeeper's wife had stood up in order to draw the beer and put it on the table before the beer haulier and the Persian woman spoke her first sentence. She was glad, she said, she had come to the larch-wood with me. This had been the first time in years that she had been with anyone other than her companion. She had found it simply impossible to speak even a single word during the walk, she was no longer used to it. There was a lot she would have liked to say but had been unable to say. In point of fact she had been living with her companion for a great many years just as silently and wordlessly. No conversation between the two of them, not the least talk. Years and years more or less wordlessly with a person, that is the Swiss, with whom she no longer had anything in common. She did not say: and from whom she could no longer detach herself, that was *my* thought. That was all, for the innkeeper's wife had sat down again by the bar and taken up her knitting and started listening again. But the Persian woman remained silent and said no more until she said goodbye. She got the innkeeper's wife to put the fur coat, which had dried in the meantime, round her shoulders and went up to her room. And left.

I had not been sure if it would be right to ask her out for a walk again the following day. I had been home all day, or more accurately downstairs, until I suddenly felt a need to distract myself with a book from my thoughts about the Persian woman, which had dominated me all the morning and the major part of the afternoon, and after a long time, certainly after weeks, when I had been unable to read anything, I had again been able to go up to my library. I had furnished the smallest upstairs room as my so-called library and so equipped it that I could do nothing else there but read, read books or study essays, for which purpose I had placed but a single chair in that room, which stood in front of the only window, a hard, by all standards uncomfortable and perfectly simple chair, the most suitable one for reading that could be imagined, thus sitting on that wooden chair by the window I could, once I had decided to do so, engross myself undisturbed in whatever reading matter I chose, that afternoon, as I remember accurately, from an edition of Schopenhauer's *The World as Will and Idea*, which I had inherited from the library of my maternal grandfather and from which I always read whenever I expected nothing else from my reading than all-round purifying pleasure. *The World as Will and Idea* had, from earliest youth, been to me the most important of all philosophical books and I have always been able to rely on its effect, that is a complete refreshment of my head. In no other book had I ever found a clearer language and an equally clear intellect, no work of literature had ever made a deeper impression on me. In the company of that book I have always been happy. But only rarely had I had the natural and intellectual preparation necessary, and only rarely therefore had I had the opportunity of being in the company of that extraordinary and truly world-determining book, because to *The World as Will and Idea* applies what applies to but a few other *supreme* books, that they reveal themselves to the reader and allow themselves to be deciphered only in a state of extreme capacity, that is receptive *capacity* and receptive *worthiness*. That capacity

I had that afternoon to the highest degree. My encounter with the Persian woman, which undoubtedly had rescued me from a not only prolonged but indeed exceedingly prolonged isolation and despair during the past few years and, in the truest meaning of the word, made myself tolerable to myself again, not least also as a consequence of my walk with her to the larch-wood, which had been a failure only if viewed from the surface but which in fact must have had the very opposite effect, had been the main reason why, after so long, I had been able to spend some time again in my library, moreover with *The World as Will and Idea*, calmed and in a pleasant frame of mind. And the last thing I had expected was that, after an hour or more with *The World as Will and Idea*, I would suddenly feel a need for my scientific studies, and I had got up and walked out of my library and unlocked the room where I had locked up my scientific studies, that is all my scientific essays and all the essays and books belonging to those scientific studies. For months I had been unable to look at those essays and essays about essays and those books and books about books because I had been in a state of deepest despair. That state was now at an end. It needs to be said at this point that over the past few years I had very often got into such a situation of absolute despair and hopelessness, probably always from the same cause, from a discontent ceaselessly and permanently gnawing me from within and paralysing and eventually deadening everything within me, and it had always been incomprehensible to me afterwards how I managed to emerge from that situation again, but the despair and hopelessness into which I had sunk with my whole being as a result of my absolute despair and hopelessness about my work, in which I had for months come to a standstill both mentally and physically, had been the worst, and I actually believe that, had the Swiss couple, and more particularly the woman friend of the Swiss, the Persian woman, not appeared here, that condition, lasting as it did the whole summer and the whole autumn, would have killed me. These states, pathological states, were naturally getting worse, I had had them for decades, initially scarcely perceptible and in an attenuated form so that they were not worth mentioning, but subsequently, with the beginning of my scientific work proper and with the real seriousness of my scientific-philosophical work, they had intensified each time and eventually revealed themselves at first as sporadic *symptoms* of illness and then finally as an illness and indeed a *severe illness*. At first I still believed in a cure for that illness, but eventually it had become pointless to hope for a cure and even the arrival of the Swiss couple did not imply a cure but only an attenuation of my state of sickness, naturally not a cure but only a suspension of the process of sickness which I had to assume had persisted for decades, just as this process of sickness persists to this day and will, I am sure, persist for the rest of my life. The Swiss couple had achieved an attenuation of the symptoms of my sickness, but of course even the Swiss couple could not cure the sickness itself, yet the Swiss couple had saved me from my absolute inability to move, and I had gone to see Moritz just as if I had surmised that they would appear at Moritz's, after all there is no such thing as even the least coincidence. Whereas in all previous severe attacks of this sickness it had been enough for me to leave my house and walk through the wood to Moritz's, it probably would not have been enough during this severe, indeed I am bound to say most severe, attack simply to go and see Moritz, and surely, during my desperate efforts that afternoon *vis-à-vis* Moritz, I had been able to see that my efforts were not leading anywhere and would not lead anywhere even though I had staked everything on that visit and had, as I have said, been determined to analyse my sickness to Moritz; my visit to Moritz, whom, as I have to admit, I have always sought out like a doctor and therefore like a life-saver, like a mind and body saver, and whom I seek out to this day whenever I am at the end of my tether, in this function which he probably does not himself realize at all, merely to go and see Moritz and pour out to him my pent-up mental and emotional garbage would have been no use that afternoon, I would quite certainly have failed in my efforts, even on my way to Moritz I had known that, despite the help of Frau Moritz, his mother, and his son, who had always looked after me in the most selfless way, that with this attack it would prove useless to go and see Moritz in the usual, often practised, manner, and I had not only felt it but *known* it, and I had, long before entering the Moritz home, reconciled myself to having foundered, finally foundered, and hence to being ruined and annihilated, and no one except a person in such a hopeless situation as myself can gauge what such total self-revelation, as I had enacted in front of Moritz, really means, that I had the courage to reveal and unveil everything concerning myself, without sparing my own person in the least and of course without sparing Moritz's person in the least either, these two, my person and his, had been a matter of complete indifference to me during that attack of mental brutality and emotional brutality and truly without the slightest thought of shielding or sparing him in my mind. The causes of this renewed and worst of all attacks of my sickness, however, are not to be sought and found in the fact that I had been overtaxed by my work in the most intolerable way and therefore been deceived and most painfully disturbed in my mind, but they were also deeply rooted in absolutely everything that was around me, in my whole environment, the immediate and the not so immediate and the more remote and the remotest environment were to be blamed for the fact that I had been precipitated into such a state of sickness, not least the baseness and the malevolence and the insidiousness of my immediate environment, which seemed increasingly and in all its manifestations to be concentrating on destroying and annihilating me, against which I had been totally powerless and in the knowledge of being powerless and helpless in the face of that destructive and annihilating will I had, in conjunction with my inability to work, that is my absolute helplessness with regard to work, partially myself caused this terrible outbreak of my sickness, and the frightful political conditions in our country and throughout Europe had perhaps triggered this catastrophe, because everything in politics was developing in precisely the opposite direction from what I had been convinced was correct and from what I am to this day convinced is correct. Political conditions at that point had suddenly deteriorated in a way which can only be described as dreadful and deadly. The endeavours of decades had been wiped out within a few weeks, and what had always been an unstable country had in effect collapsed within a few weeks, dim-wittedness, greed and hypocrisy were suddenly again at the helm just as in the worst times of the worst regime, and those in power were once again ruthlessly working towards the extermination of the intellect. A hostility to the intellect, perceived by me for some years, had reached a new repugnant peak, the people, or more correctly the popular masses, had been encouraged by the rulers to engage in mind murder and whipped up into head hunting and mind hunting. Everything had once more overnight become *dictatorial* and I had for weeks, indeed for months, experienced in my own person how they were after the heads of those who thought. Smug philistinism, prepared to sweep out of its way anything it did not like, and that meant mainly anything that was head or mind, had the upper hand and was suddenly again being used by the government and not only by this government but by all European governments. The masses, clinging to bellies and possessions, were on the march against the heads and against the minds.

Anyone thinking must be mistrusted and must be persecuted, that is the old slogan according to which they are once more acting in the most terrible manner. The newspapers speak a distasteful language, the distasteful language they have always spoken but which, during the past few decades, they had spoken only with lowered voices, which suddenly they no longer had any reason to do, almost without exception they were posturing like the people in order to please the people, those mind murderers. Dreams of a world of the mind had been betrayed during these weeks and thrown on the popular refuse heap. The voices of the intellect had fallen silent. Heads were ducking. There was now only brutality, vileness and infamy. This circumstance, in conjunction with the standstill of my work, was bound to result in a deep depression of my entire being and to weaken me in a way which eventually led to the worst outbreak of my sickness. I had always been dependent on everything and when, all of a sudden and then more and more seriously and alarmingly, everything was getting worse, this the worst of all my attacks of sickness had been bound to come. Admittedly, if someone lives in the country, that is in retirement in the country because he has to live there, because, like me, he is forced, as a consequence of his severe illness, to lead such an ultimately dreadful life in the country, such *horrors* strike him more profoundly than one who lives in the city, because the person who, like me, lives in the country with intellectual work is continually and in the most extreme manner concentrated on that intellectual work, and because a person like myself finds his receptivity for everything else weighing upon his head and therefore upon his intellect and upon his mind with far greater and more lasting intensity. The times that I have regretted having moved out to the country, if only I had stayed in the city, because I am not a countryman even if my parents were country people, I am not a countryman, even though the country is so familiar to me, but the city is just as familiar to me as the country and I love the city better than the country, which most of the time I hate because most of the time it has tormented me, tormented and humiliated me as far as I can think back, and baseness and infamy are far greater in the country than in the city, just as brutality in the country is much greater, and always shameless, and the country, by contrast to the city, is totally mindless. Two main reasons, not to mention hundreds of secondary reasons, made me move out to the country, first, because the doctor told me that in view of my lung disease I could only survive in the country, and second, because I was willing to sacrifice the city to my studies, that is to my scientific work. But I have paid a very high price, I have paid the top price. Living in the country I have always felt to be a punishment, because everything within me has always been so disposed that it was ultimately disposed against the country. Each day I have lived in the country I have had to tell myself that I was living in the country for the sake of my scientific studies and of my lungs, that is quite simply for the sake of being able to exist. Life in the country, to a person like myself, is the most dreadful kind of life, if indeed in my case there can be any talk of a kind of life, probably not. Because I live in the country, I tell myself every day, I live, I exist, had I stayed in the city I should no longer live, no longer exist, but this is probably a totally and utterly nonsensical idea, because surely it is of no consequence whether or not I live and therefore exist, but if such a thought is present it must be thought through to the end, I believe. And every day, here in the country, I am mercilessly confronted with the thought that my sacrifice is a pointless sacrifice because my existence is a pathological, a sick one, and my work is useless and a failure. But I lack the courage to put an end to this and to similar thoughts and hence to myself. I have always lacked that courage. All my life I have always

65

considered suicide but have never been able to execute that suicide. And then, after the arrival of the Swiss couple and above all the Persian woman, who, I do not know for what reason, had fascinated me from the first moment, for many crucial reasons, probably for many, possibly for hundreds and thousands, of, to me, life-saving reasons, which, concentrated in the Persian woman, had been discernible by me and at once highly useful to me, I have quite simply, in the most ridiculous and shameless, and also in the most depressing, manner, once more clung to my life and to my existence. This has always been distasteful and simultaneously also doubly depressing. But one day, I keep saying, I shall do what I have to do one day, I shall commit suicide, because my life and my existence have become pointless, and to continue that absolute pointlessness and again to continue it is senseless. I asked myself how it had been possible that on the very next day after my encounter with the Swiss couple I could approach my scientific writings again, that I was able to walk upstairs to my library and to read in *The World as Will and Idea*, and eventually even to consider taking up my scientific studies again, to resume them where I had to leave off more than six months before. I asked myself how it had been possible, one day after the encounter with the Swiss couple, to be downright hungry for life, because none of all my earlier attacks had had any such purifying effect and had only been able to attenuate my state but not to extinguish it, and I think that it was the enormous intensity of that attack which produced this extraordinary release. But this release, of course, could only last a few days, after two or three weeks I had been back in a deep depression, but that is another story. The Swiss couple, in conjunction with Moritz and his family, had brought about a prolonged, indeed the most prolonged, period without an attack, never before had I had such a long interval between two attacks without being totally at the mercy of my sickness, in other words being almost entirely liberated from that sickness, as during the period when I went for walks with the Persian woman and that is the period under discussion here; had I not come to the country that sickness, which logically got worse with my existence in the country, could not have developed in that devastating manner, but had I stayed in the city I would no longer be existing at all, and therefore this new thought, whether I would not have done better to stay in the city and not move out to the country, is senseless. Perhaps it would have been better if I had not come up against Moritz but against some other estate agent and if I had bought a place somewhere quite different, not this ruin which possibly has meant my misfortune. Time and again I had blamed my sickness on the damp and cold walls of this building, on the fact that I, moreover entirely by my own decision, have existed in this building and still exist in it today, a building which is the worst conceivable for my health. Thus, on the one hand, I had left the city because the city is bad for my health and, on the other, found myself in a building which possibly is a lot worse for my health than even the city. With these thoughts, which I have kept thinking, off and on, for many long years, I have naturally not been able to come to any conclusion. Quite possibly I had also been wrecked by my own work on that building, because I have rebuilt the ruin with my own hands and virtually entirely without outside help. For years and years doing nothing but masonry and masonry and again masonry, and as a result weakening myself in the most irresponsible manner, possibly provided the trigger for these, subsequently even more severe, outbreaks of my sickness. It should, moreover, be realized that this region is one of the gloomiest in the whole country, and that the people existing here exactly match this gloomy and basically people-repelling landscape, the people here are like the landscape. I had certainly come to a landscape which does not suit me, one in which I *can* never feel at home, if words such as *at home* are permissible at all. Thus I have always had a defensive relationship towards that landscape, on the other hand this very point had been a reason for purchasing that ruin, that the landscape in which my house stands has a great deal of similarity with the landscape from which I come. But none of these thoughts leads anywhere, and the more I pursue them the more confused everything becomes. If even I had such terrible difficulties on coming to this neighbourhood, how much greater must be the difficulties which the Persian woman now encounters in this neighbourhood, in a, to her, entirely new and certainly merciless situation, I thought. On the one hand I thought that the Swiss would make things easier for her because it is well known that two people can cope with such a problem more easily than one on his own, and on the other hand I was not sure whether the Swiss, and more particularly the nature of the Swiss, that is the character of the Swiss, would not make things a lot more difficult for the Persian woman. We keep trying to uncover backgrounds but we do not get any farther, we merely complicate and disjoint even more what is already complicated and disjointed enough. We look for someone responsible for our fate, which, most of the time, if only we are honest, we might simply call our misfortune. We brood about what we should have done differently or better or what perhaps we should not have done, because we are doomed to do so, but it does not lead anywhere. The disaster was inevitable, is what we then say and for a while, if only a short while, we are quiet. Then we start all over again asking questions and probing and probing until we have gone half crazy. We constantly look for someone responsible, or for several persons responsible, in order to make things bearable for ourselves at least for a moment, and naturally, if we are honest, we invariably end up with ourselves. We have reconciled ourselves to the fact that we have to exist, even though most of the time *against* our will, because we have no other choice, and only because we have again and again reconciled ourselves to this fact, every day and every moment anew, can we progress at all. And where we are progressing to, we have, if we are honest, known all our lives, to death, except that most of the time we are careful not to admit it. And because we have that certainty of doing nothing other than progressing towards death and because we realize what that means, we try to employ all kinds of aids to divert us from that realization, and thus, if only we look closely, we see in this world nothing except people continually and all their lives engaged in such a diversion. This process, which is the principal process in most people, naturally weakens or accelerates the whole development towards death. This thought had come to me as, sitting in my corner seat in Moritz's box-file room on the afternoon the Swiss couple arrived, I was contemplating and observing the Swiss couple. All these people, no matter who they are, are dominated, I thought, by that process of diverting their attention from the death which inescapably stands before them. Everything about everybody is nothing but diversion from death. It is surprising that I have been able to develop such thoughts especially to Moritz, that I have been able to speak to Moritz about such thoughts of death. So long as we have but a single person near us with whom we can ultimately talk about *everything* we can hold out, otherwise we cannot. I now had the Persian woman for such thoughts and for talk arising from such thoughts, and I was not deceived. Although, on the day after my first encounter with the Persian woman, I had not intended to leave my house under any circumstances because suddenly I found it possible again to enjoy all its rooms, and indeed in each of those rooms, until then closed to me because of their atrociousness, I had, during the day, spent at least as much time as it took me to study thoroughly the purposefulness of every one of those rooms and in fact to enjoy them, I had gone to my library and to the room where I kept my scientific papers, and again with the same thought, that I now was once more able to exist in that house without being constantly in fear, no matter of what, I suddenly decided to get outside and run away, I did not care in what direction, and I rushed out of the house and across the wet meadows and into the wood, but in a totally different state of mind from the day before, not in fear and terror but with confidence. There had indeed occurred a significant calming of my whole mind and a clearing of my head, benefits which I would not have dreamt of thinking about a mere twenty-four hours earlier, and I ran and ran and kept making detours in order to enjoy as long as possible that state of being free, of having escaped my dreadful sickness and of being in a position to exist without that painful certainty that I was incurably sick. I had run through the fields and through the woods to the point of total exhaustion that evening and all of a sudden I saw everything in those fields and in those woods with different eyes, suddenly it no longer destroyed or annihilated anything within me, and even the people whom, even though I avoided them, I was bound to meet did not make such a terrible impression on me as the day before. My existence seemed to be once again possible. Although I knew that this state of once again being able to exist would not last long, this did not then trouble me. That sudden light-headedness, that sudden light-limbedness, that complete independence of all pains and of all conceivable humiliations on this earth quite simply made me happy and I was not compelled to reflect *upon myself*. In the early evening, in that state of mind I had not gone home but to Moritz's house, I had knocked and I was immediately let in by Frau Moritz and I was allowed to go up to the box-file room and sit down in my corner seat. Moritz was not in but would very soon return, Frau Moritz said, and, left alone by Frau Moritz who always had domestic jobs to do, I had the leisure calmly to regard everything that could be seen from my corner seat, with the calm that is necessary even for quite ordinary objects to be found in a room, and which I had not had for a long time. I was able to indulge quite *naturally* in the observation of the objects in Moritz's box-file room without being crushed and stifled by them, for which, after all, they are not basically intended but which those objects in Moritz's box-file room had always been able to do to me, because very frequently, and almost invariably in my sick states, I had had the feeling in that very room

73

that the objects were crushing and stifling me, but now I could contemplate them calmly and, in my observation, was left alone by them. There was no thought preventing me from regarding those objects, cabinets, chairs, table, desk and so on in such a way that all these objects appeared to me as *natural and not in the least terrible* as they had mostly seemed to me, as indeed most of the time I have to regard all objects as if they were crushing and stifling me. In that observation, and while hearing from below the sounds of Frau Moritz working, I had reduced all those objects in Moritz's box-file room to their natural functions, reduced cabinets, chairs, table, desk to their actual functions, and not allowed them to hit me over the head or terrify me. To think of what I had seen in that box-file room, in that, to me, invariably notorious box-file room, whenever I used to look around me I had invariably looked at the worst horror and atrociousness. I had always seen the whole shamelessness and appallingness of the world in that box-file room whenever I had looked around. But now I succeeded in seeing the whole box-file room as it was, as a pleasant, a very pleasant, friendly room exactly suited to Moritz's office work, with two large windows opening to the west and therefore always filled with good air and nearly always with light. There could be some argument about the furnishings, but surely I have no right to question Moritz's taste with regard to the box-file room at the very time I am sitting in it, I thought. And then I saw the whole scene of the previous day before me: Moritz in his felt slippers, the Swiss in his grey department-store suit, the Persian woman, although it was in fact pleasantly warm in the box-file room, in her high-collared fur coat, which presumably was a Persian lamb coat from her native country. I actually now saw myself sitting in the corner seat, as though I was viewing myself from the side of the room opposite my corner seat, admittedly silent while the others were talking, utterly exhausted from the eruption and attack of my sickness, for a very long time unable to utter a single connected sentence, only now and then a word, a little affirmative remark to a question directly addressed to me by Moritz, nothing else, simply in a feeling of total exhaustion. That was the previous day. Now the box-file room was empty of those people but I, sitting in my corner seat, could bring them back into the box-file room if I wished to, or make them disappear, just as I pleased, I was enjoying that toing and froing and persisted with it until Moritz came home, I could hear him in the vestibule, he always spoke loudly and clearly, as, stepping into the vestibule, he slipped off his winter overcoat and inquired about dinner. Frau Moritz immediately told him that I was here, in the box-file room. Without further ado Moritz very quickly appeared in the box-file room. He opened a bottle of wine and sat down facing me. How different the present situation was from that a mere twenty-four hours earlier. Now, quite calm, I wanted to hear from Moritz details about the Swiss couple, how he had come to meet them and of course also why he had never spoken about them, though they would undoubtedly have interested me more than anyone else, why he had never as much as mentioned them, considering that he always mentioned the people he met, especially interesting ones. He now reminded me that for more than three months I had not been to see him and that, for that reason alone, he had not been able to say anything to me about the Swiss couple. It had not seemed quite as long as that to me since I had been to see Moritz, but he was right. The thought that I had cut myself off for three months and during those three months never once left my house, or certainly not my property, frightened me. Also the fact that for three months I had in fact not spoken to anybody, it had seemed a terribly long time to me but not as long as three months, but I should have been aware from the reaction of the innkeeper's wife the moment I entered the inn to call for the Persian woman. Did she not say she had thought I was dead? That is what people say when they see someone again whom they have not seen for a much longer than *normal* period. She had said she had thought that I had died, and I had heard those words and yet not heard them. In actual fact I had not left my house for three months and had lived off my supplies. For three months I had lived at home full of fear, and this had of course been noticed and that was why people, when they saw me outside my house again for the first time, had looked at me so oddly. They had all regarded me more oddly than ever before. Now that I had lived in my house for three months in a kind of self-incarceration I had become even more sinister to them than before and that was how they reacted when they met me. As I was walking up through the village to meet the Persian woman they had followed me with their eyes as they had never followed me before, even more mistrustfully, even more suspiciously. But I must not allow myself to be upset now. I told Moritz that, prior to his return home, I had been totally absorbed in the observation of his office, of the box-file room, *in complete calm*, I said, *quite calmly without the least excitement*. He reported on a drive to Kirchdorf, which had taken up the whole of

77

his afternoon but on which he had come across a lot of new things. New plots of land, new people. In Kirchdorf itself he had bought an old carbine dating back to the year forty-two, for a bargain price, which pleased him. He went out and returned with the carbine and held it up, and I would not have put it past him to fire it through the window. However, he lowered it again and took it apart and explained to me how it worked and stood it in the corner. This very situation might have induced him to tell me one of his war stories, which I could no longer bear to hear, but he did not do so, he probably was too tired. The people in this region, he said, were absolutely the vilest he knew, they forced one to treat them with the same vileness they used at every opportunity. Basically they deserved no better than to be exploited and deceived. Again and again in their presence one forgot that they were simply humans. Such trips, on which he always experienced new instances of human meanness and vileness and in which I very often participated in the past, if only to get away from my work and from my house, from my work prison and my existential prison, but also in order, like him, to meet new people and new characters and new abominations and monstrosities, had always both exhausted and refreshed him. It is a long time since I had last participated in his expeditions, it seems to me, that way I came to know the whole country down to its farthest corner, all those people and their conditions. And I have never in my life learned more about people than on those reconnaissance trips with Moritz, whose life's ambition it was, and still is, to be a broker of plots and properties of all kinds, to discover sellers and buyers and to do business with them. And he always only did good business. And only rarely had he allowed himself to be induced to commit a minor or major, though never criminal, deception. Moritz is a man of the most sterling character I have ever met in my life, even though the opposite, and indeed nothing but the opposite, was always and everywhere said, and is being said, about him. Hardly anyone had ever known him or seen through him better than I had. Just because he had been despised by everyone, and actually even hated, I had been attracted to him, I have always had a predilection for the despised and hated. He conducted his business no differently from the way others conducted theirs, he bought and sold, and buys and sells, plots of land and properties just as workmen perform their work or peasants cultivate their pastures and fields. Or the way the priest says Mass. Only with a little more intelligence and a little more insolence. That in doing so he made more money than the others did in their businesses was in the nature of his occupation. They envied him everything and persecuted him with their envy day and night. Because of that they all seemed to be repugnant and base. They cursed him and they cursed his wife and his mother and his son. The word *dealer* had been stamped on him by everyone in the vilest manner. But they were not too fastidious to do business with him and often they had been ready for such dirty business that he had to refuse it because it had been too dirty for him. Whenever they wanted to do business, peasants, workers, quite simply owners of property, their whole infamy emerged. He had never been as infamous as they were. His origins were of the humblest. He never denied them and he allowed himself no luxury of any kind. For that, admittedly, his deals were not big enough. I know of no one who looked after his family better than him. That he had sold the water-logged and cold and, for most of the day, dark meadow to the Swiss couple as a building plot for their declining years – who could blame him for that, seeing that he had had to wait so many years for a buyer of that meadow and that over the years he had conducted hundreds or more of interested clients across the cemetery and through the wood to see the meadow, to no avail. His profit from that deal was justified. No matter how much the Swiss couple had paid for the meadow, it was they who had wanted it. Replying to my question Moritz said that the Swiss couple had responded to one of his advertisements in the *Neue Zürcher Zeitung* and had, towards the end of August, come straight from Switzerland and that, having met them at the station, he had taken them straight away across the cemetery and through the wood to see the meadow, and they had instantly bought it. It had not taken them a quarter-hour to make up their minds, he said, which had reminded him, Moritz, of my own purchase of my property, because I too had bought the ruin and the land on which it stood within ten minutes. The Swiss couple had briefly glanced at the meadow and had agreed to buy, whereupon he had gone with the Swiss couple to the inn to draw up the sales contract. In the course of that he, Moritz, had not omitted to draw the Swiss couple's attention to the disadvantages of the meadow as a building plot. But the Swiss couple were not to be shaken in their decision to buy the meadow. Indeed he, Moritz, had taken pleasure in enumerating more drawbacks and disadvantages with regard to the meadow than the meadow actually possessed, all in vain. Ownership of the meadow had been transferred to the Swiss couple and, as was the custom with his

81

business transactions, Moritz had first treated the Swiss couple to drinks at the inn and additionally invited them home for dinner. No one cooks as well as Frau Moritz. The whole evening that I made their acquaintance the Swiss had time and again raved about the Moritz cuisine, as I remember. There had been no argument about the price, Moritz said. Although the Swiss have a reputation for never paying the asking price, they paid up without argument. It had never happened to him, Moritz, before that buyers who had made an, at least in his opinion, indubitably bad buy had subsequently been *totally* delighted with it. He had wanted to tell me about the deal with the Swiss couple immediately after its conclusion, but he had found himself, Moritz said, in front of a locked door. He had not wished to impose on me or to disturb me. That I had not been to his house for such a long time, that is for three months, he had attributed to some resentment between the two of us, which he had been unable to explain. One day I would turn up again, he had thought. But there was no question of any resentment, I had merely withdrawn and locked myself in so I could be alone with my dejection and with my increasingly intensifying depressions, with my sickness. That this state of affairs had lasted for three months, if not longer, was now a terrible thought to me. I was exceedingly interested in the Swiss couple, I said to Moritz. I regarded their intention to settle here as an exceptionally useful benefit, and I already visualized the Swiss couple as ideal conversational neighbours, not so much the Swiss himself, more his woman friend, the Persian woman. That which I had been missing here for so many years I might possibly find in the Swiss couple very soon, people with whom intellectual contact was possible. I said to Moritz that the Persian woman interested me more than any other person *in the recent past*, I did not say *for years*, I deliberately only said *in the recent past*, her sensitivity, her undoubtedly high degree of culture. Above all I had, all those years, missed a so-called foreign-language person. And the distance between my house and the house of the Swiss couple was just right, not too far, not too near, I could see myself paying regular visits to the Swiss couple. With the Swiss there might very well be good conversation about *anything real and normal*, I thought, and with his woman friend surely a *philosophical* one. As I knew by then, the Swiss woman was interested in music, of which she seemed to know a great deal. Even at my first encounter with her a great many indicative concepts and terms had been dropped, and she had mentioned Schubert, and above all Schumann, and

I loved Schumann in particular, and I had, over the past few years, concerned myself very intensively with Schumann in particular. I loved people who, like the Persian woman, declared, moreover in everything they said even if they did not utter it, that they could not exist without music. And philosophy, having studied philosophy, was nothing unfamiliar to her from the outset. I had always been fond of so-called philosophizing persons, not philosophers proper, whom I encountered in my life, and who had nothing to do with the real philosophers, whose schoolmaster philosophy and therefore philosophical twaddle had always repelled me. The present is no age for philosophers, all those so labelled nowadays are in fact labelled thus erroneously and totally misleadingly, they are nothing but common dull-witted anti-sensitive regurgitators of philosophy, who all make a livelihood from publishing hundreds and thousands of stale ideas at second or third or fourth hand, in university lecture rooms and in the book trade. There is no contemporary philosopher. But there is such a thing as the philosophizing person, and I would describe myself as such a philosophizing person, and the Persian woman probably was also a philosophizing person. But of course every philosopher is also only a philosophizing person. When the time comes, I said to Moritz,

I shall go to the Swiss couple for a musical conversation, and the other way about the Persian woman will come to me for a philosophical one. Then those winter evenings, which begin at four o'clock, will not seem so long. Originally Moritz had intended to take the Swiss couple to an altogether different plot of land, but on the way to that plot they had suddenly come to the meadow and Moritz, without the least hope of being able to sell the meadow to the Swiss couple, had shown them the meadow, and the Swiss couple, or more accurately the Swiss, had there and then decided on the meadow and had not wished to view any other plot. That buyers would buy a predictably quite unsellable plot, and moreover instantly, without wishing to view any other plot, he, Moritz, had never before experienced. The Swiss had immediately struck Moritz as a *financially sound buyer*, his decision to buy the plot had been taken by him totally uninfluenced by Moritz, on the contrary, he, Moritz, had suggested to the Swiss that he should perhaps view another plot first, but the Swiss had declined to do so, although it was always advantageous, before buying, to consider more than one offer, the Swiss was not to be moved from his decision, and Moritz eventually had entirely *yielded* to the decision of the Swiss, this was his actual word reflecting his giving in to

85

the Swiss, and the Swiss had told him, Moritz, that he had, always with his woman friend, viewed *hundreds if not thousands of plots*, that reportedly was what the Swiss had exclaimed to Moritz, but now he had had enough of all that building-plot viewing and had in fact found his ideal plot, and he had urged Moritz to speed up the paper work and had asked him to walk back at once through the wood into the village and to the inn, so the sales contract could be drawn up, which he could then sign, and with the signature on that sales contract a long period of searching for a building plot, which had been getting on his nerves for a long time, would be at an end, and no matter how strange or indeed questionable his, the Swiss's, mode of action, that is his exceedingly rapid and actually bafflingly rapid decision concerning the plot, that is the meadow, may seem to Moritz, he would not change his decision, and the three of them had, without even, as is customary in the purchase of a plot, even once pacing out the plot, that is the three-thousand or three-and-a-half-thousand-metre large meadow, returned; admittedly the woman friend of the Swiss had been anxious, because she was cold, to leave the meadow at once and to conclude the purchase, but, according to Moritz, there had probably been no need for the agreement of the woman friend of the

Swiss, and the Swiss, Moritz said, would certainly have bought the meadow even against
the will of his companion, he, Moritz, had had
that impression as indeed he had the impression
generally that his woman friend had no influence at all on the Swiss, even though it was
clear that, some years back, she must have had
a very major influence on the Swiss. In fact
everything about the Swiss, everything that the
Swiss had become, must surely have been the
product of his woman friend, I had thought so
at my very first encounter with the Swiss
couple, that especially the Swiss's whole professional career as an engineer and builder of
power stations, and above all as a celebrity,
was the product of his woman friend, such
women as the woman friend of the Swiss come
together with men like the Swiss and turn them
into celebrities, they perceive what, using all
possible efforts and contrivances, may be made
of such a man and they achieve their goal when
by their endeavours they make such a man, a
basically and naturally quite unambitious,
indeed in his disposition lethargic, man, into a
celebrity, not and never over a period of years
but by quite simply, from the very moment of
their coming upon one another and coming
together, by forcing him into a hard and cold
career. The Swiss had quite obviously been
forced into such a career by the Persian

woman, who had come across him in the thir-
ties, as quite a young student, and the calcu-
lation which the Persian woman had made had
come off, at least as far as the career of the
Swiss was concerned, because there was no
doubt that the Swiss was a top figure in his
field, this the Swiss couple had, at the very
outset and instantly, documented not only by
their own remarks but by all kinds of papers,
photographs, and so on, illustrating his career.
Kings and queens and state presidents, Moritz
had said to me, shake hands at the inauguration
of such colossal power-station buildings only
with men who had actually built those power
stations and in point of fact, so I thought, there
was in the physiognomy of the Swiss everything of which he and his woman friend, the
Persian woman, had spoken to me at our first
encounter. Besides, there was no reason whatever for mistrusting or disbelieving what the
Swiss and his woman friend had told me, and
although, in the company of people, I am permanently on the look-out for contradictions, I
was unable to discover any such contradictions
about the Swiss couple. What this man, the
Swiss, is saying is authentic, I had thought,
and I had been equally convinced of the truth
of what his woman friend had said. Moritz
certainly never ceased to be amazed at these
famous people who had suddenly turned up at

his place. The Swiss, according to Moritz, as he was for the first time standing in the meadow he had so precipitately bought, had exclaimed: *This is the first piece of land that I own!*, this had greatly impressed Moritz who could not understand that there were people, more or less like the Swiss couple, evidently very wealthy people, who, at a fairly advanced point in their lives, had never yet owned a piece of land. As a real-estate agent Moritz was bound to assume that anyone with any claim at all to social acceptability possessed some real estate or at least a property corresponding to some real estate, an adult being who possessed no real estate was difficult for Moritz to envisage and indeed such beings were basically not human beings in his eyes, and so he had made it his ambition, as it were his life's ambition, to make those, as he saw it, pitiable real-estate-less and property-less wretches, who to his real-estate agent's eyes were not human beings at all, into human beings by selling them real estate or properties or by at least trying, time and again, to sell them such real estate or properties. The Swiss had told Moritz that among a dozen advertisements deserving consideration it had been the very one which he, Moritz, had placed in the *Neue Zürcher Zeitung* that had exercised the greatest magnetism on him, the Swiss, and this for Moritz had been a reason for even greater respect for the Swiss. It appeared that the Swiss couple had expected this region to be a serene one, because everywhere and throughout the world it is described as serene, and they had been surprised to find it so gloomy. But that discovery had merely confirmed them in their resolution to buy the meadow and to settle in just this gloomy region, the very gloominess of the landscape had, on the contrary, confirmed them in their intention. For decades the Swiss couple had lived mainly in Asia and in South America, where the sun shines practically without a break, *in serene landscapes*, and this had in the long run produced in them a weariness of such serene landscapes and regions, for decades, the Swiss had said to Moritz, they had been burnt dry by the sun and they now longed for a cool and shady spot. This of course was the very opposite of what all other buyers of building plots and properties invariably exclusively seek. Even during their walk from the village through the wood Moritz had had the impression of leading the Swiss couple, or at least the Swiss, into a natural setting agreeable to them or at least to him. The Swiss had drawn a breath of relief as soon as it had become dark and dank in the wood and his steps at that moment had become faster, and that had given him, Moritz, the idea of quite simply showing the Swiss couple the water-logged meadow to begin with, the one he had shown to hundreds of people before, without avail. The Swiss had already been delighted by the damp and cold wood and it had not worried him that the way to the wood led through the cemetery, Moritz said, and he, Moritz, had of course walked ahead and had cleared the path for the Swiss couple. In contrast to the Swiss's enthusiasm, Moritz said, he had been struck by the taciturnity of his companion, his woman friend, who on the way to the water-logged meadow had fallen some distance behind and basically, for the duration of the whole viewing of the meadow, had remained taciturn if not altogether silent, that was what had struck Moritz in particular, that the Persian woman, whom he, Moritz, had of course also taken for a Swiss, had, for the duration of the viewing, given him an impression of complete indifference. She had watched everything from a greater, to her mind probably favourable, distance and had not interfered at all, not said a word. That was what had struck Moritz as peculiar, that during that viewing the Swiss had done what he chose without, so it had seemed to Moritz, taking the slightest notice of his companion, he had not even once asked her a question, and not even put to her the crucial question of whether or not he should buy the plot which Moritz and I invariably called *the water-logged meadow*. Surely the building plot, so Moritz thought, was intended for the two of them, and it was therefore incomprehensible why the decision to buy the meadow should have been taken by the Swiss alone. When the Swiss had bought the meadow and, Moritz said, they had shaken hands on it, the three had wordlessly gone back to the village and to the inn. Moritz had been unable to say anything because he was still stunned by the, to him extremely odd, way this plot had been sold, and the Swiss couple likewise, for some other reason known only to them. There had not been the least argument about the price, Moritz said, not the least discussion, quite against Moritz's expectation who, taking into consideration the manner and deportment of the Swiss, had been prepared for a lengthy debate on the purchasing price. It had been one of those August days which always favoured a sale, the day the Swiss had come to Moritz, he, Moritz, had a good nose for whether the weather was favourable or unfavourable for business, and the weather in which he had sold the water-logged meadow to the Swiss couple had been sale-favourable weather, on certain days, under the effect of the weather, almost anything could be sold and on other days nothing, again under the effect of the weather.

A good businessman, Moritz said, always had to take into consideration the momentary weather pattern and to ask himself if that weather pattern was or was not favourable for initiating or concluding a deal. Yet very few of those engaging in business were taking this vital circumstance into consideration or acting accordingly. Moritz had been afraid of the arrival of the Swiss couple because he had believed that he had nothing useful to offer them, because everyone expects the Swiss to make the highest demands imaginable, and the Swiss, moreover, are inaccessible to no matter what arguments from the very start of no matter what negotiations, more particularly of negotiations about the sale of real estate or other properties. Initiating deals with Swiss clients and negotiating them and eventually closing the deals was the most difficult thing that could happen to a non-Swiss partner, Moritz said. But while he had prepared himself for what he called a tough negotiating climate and had fully expected to encounter it, the deal he concluded with the Swiss couple had eventually been one of the easiest deals which he, Moritz, had ever concluded. It often happens that the reality of an event proves to be diametrically opposed to the mental picture one had of it beforehand. The moment the three of them had sat down at the inn and Moritz had got down to drafting the sales contract, the Swiss, Moritz said, had produced from his overcoat pocket a plan which proved to be the plan of the house which the Swiss intended to build on the meadow plot he had only just bought, and Moritz now observed that this, too, had never happened to him before, that the buyer of a building plot, even before he knew where he was going to put his house, had already drawn up the plan of that house, surely it was always the other way round, that first of all the plot was decided upon and only then the plan for the building to be erected on that plot drawn up, Moritz's astonishment must have been enormous, at first he had not believed that the plan which the Swiss had suddenly, while Moritz was drawing up the sales contract, produced from his overcoat pocket could be the very plan of the house that was to be put on the meadow plot purchased only half an hour before, but the Swiss had immediately convinced him of the truth of what he was asserting and what Moritz could not believe, by spreading the plan out on the table and beginning to explain details of that plan. He, the Swiss, had designed that plan as much as three years ago, in South America, or to be precise in a small place near Caracas, the Venezuelan capital, and he had been carrying that plan around with him for the past three years, the plan was actually, probably due to its being continuously pulled out of that overcoat pocket and replaced in it, much the worse for wear, Moritz said. In Caracas, Moritz said, the Swiss had decided, as he seems to have emphatically pointed out to Moritz, to settle *in Austria and not in Switzerland*, and Moritz believed that this was for tax reasons. At the request of the woman friend of the Swiss the innkeeper's wife had, though at first reluctantly, eventually lit a very good fire because the bar parlour had been cold and unfriendly as is so often the case towards the end of August, and on that occasion he, Moritz, had been struck by the Persian woman's great susceptibility to cold, by the fact that the woman, although there was of course no reason for that, had worn her Persian lamb coat all the time since her arrival and that she had turned up the collar of the Persian lamb coat, which had induced Moritz to ask her if she had a cold, which however she denied. Such women, who had lived virtually all their lives in warm countries, invariably feel the cold in our climate and Moritz, too, from the very beginning had the impression that the woman friend of the Swiss was suffering from a perpetual fear of freezing to death. The Swiss had no problem at all with our climate, he seemed to be in excellent health, which, however, very soon proved to be an illusion because the Swiss suffered from serious gall bladder and kidney complaints and moreover, like so many of his professional, or quite simply business, colleagues, had ruined his lungs by smoking. Moritz had also been amazed by the detail in which the Swiss had designed his house, that plan had not only differed from other, locally customary, plans of houses by its downright bold peculiarity but it was also distinguished by the *greatest possible precision*. Every line and every caption and numbering in it were proof that the plan was a Swiss plan and designed by a thoroughly Swiss head. It was instantly obvious that this plan was a plan designed by a person feeling and thinking in highly idiosyncratic and totally egotistical feelings and thoughts. Not the least trace of any feminine influence. When Moritz had wondered whether the kitchen was not perhaps in an unfavourable position, because as he, Moritz, now visualized the plot on which this house would stand, it meant that the kitchen window would open on to the wood, the Swiss had merely laughed and remarked that the plan had been *repeatedly and thoroughly thought through by him over a period of three years* and that everything in that plan, his plan, *answered* his requirements, he had not said *their*, that is his and his woman friend's requirements, he had said it answered his requirements, which had struck Moritz as particularly inconsiderate. The Swiss, moreover, had always referred to *his* purchase of the plot, not that *both of them, that is he and his woman friend,* had bought the plot. With his advertisement in the *Neue Zürcher Zeitung* having unexpectedly proved so successful, he, Moritz, had decided to place further advertisements in the *Neue Zürcher Zeitung*, although he had been firmly determined never to place an advertisement in the *Neue Zürcher Zeitung* again because for a whole year none of his advertisements in that paper had produced the least result, and now his final advertisement in the *Neue Zürcher Zeitung* had resulted in a vast success. He had sold the water-logged meadow which had been unsellable for more than a decade. While drawing up the sales contract Moritz had speculated about the real relationship between the Swiss couple, whom at first, quite naturally, he had taken for a married couple, which, however, had soon been corrected by the Swiss couple, the Swiss having used the term *woman friend* to Moritz. He, the Swiss, wanted to return to Switzerland that very night, he had told Moritz, in order to make important preparations for the start of construction, to make inquiries concerning the most favourable building materials, because the Swiss had immediately voiced his doubts to Moritz about the quality of Austrian materials, as well as making derogatory remarks regarding the cost of such materials in Austria, the only question was how to transport those materials from Switzerland across the frontier into Austria, above all how to avoid customs duty so artfully and unobtrusively that he would save himself amazingly high costs, as the Swiss had been able very quickly to work out at the table. Everything about and in that building was to be of the best and the most expensive, but he, the Swiss, had never yet in his life, no matter for what, paid the top price. The Swiss had requested Moritz to reflect on how he, the Swiss, could find the best and the cheapest workmen, and Moritz had immediately promised him the ideal workmen, the so-called *ethnic Germans*, with whom he had frequently collaborated. The Swiss had instantly understood that the so-called ethnic Germans were good and cheap workers. The Swiss, born in Zug and brought up in Berne, where he attended the local engineering college, had, Moritz said, been not only pleased but downright fascinated by the fact that his newly purchased plot had a very marked slope, the very circumstance that had always been the reason for its unsellability. He, Moritz, had also drawn the attention of the Swiss to the high degree of dampness of the plot, which the Swiss, so honestly enlightened by Moritz, did not seem to mind in the least. In winter, Moritz had moreover revealed to the Swiss, it was sometimes altogether impossible to get to the plot, snow clearance was impossible under those circumstances. That warning had not affected the Swiss either. Besides, it was not to everybody's liking to approach the plot through the cold and virtually always dark wood, Moritz had said to the Swiss, Moritz said. They, the Swiss couple, would probably have to stock up with food supplies for several weeks, like it or not, because they might well be unable to get out of their house and into the village. The Swiss, Moritz said, was not to be shaken. Moritz had suggested that the Swiss, in agreement with the proprietors of the wood, might agree on some lifetime lease in order, for instance, to have a proper access road built through the wood, but the Swiss, Moritz said, had rejected his suggestion. He was satisfied with the conditions prevailing at the moment, he would not dream of building an access road. But in winter, Moritz had told the Swiss, everything round his property was just a quagmire. This, too, had failed to impress the Swiss in the least. During all that time his woman friend had been sitting at the table, wordlessly sipping tea and smoking cigarettes, still wearing her Persian lamb coat, almost huddled into that Persian lamb coat, Moritz said, and continually looking at the table top, or rather at a single point on the table top. Moritz had a simple, regular hand, which gives the sales contracts completed by him a clean and agreeable confidence-inspiring appearance, that was what the Swiss had told him, Moritz, after he had read once through the sales contract which Moritz had slowly and deliberately filled in, and Moritz had of course noted that the Swiss had complimented him on his handwriting but had otherwise not commented at all on the contents of the sales contract. Moritz had scarcely believed his eyes when the Swiss had actually put his signature to the contract. Such smooth transactions, Moritz said, came his way only once in every few years. On the following day the Swiss had already put the full purchase price on Moritz's desk. The Swiss, as I happen to know, prefer to pay cash, and mostly do, and whenever possible avoid a roundabout transaction through a bank. The Swiss had, in point of fact, returned to Switzerland the following night, leaving his woman friend at the inn. He, Moritz, thinking that she could not be left alone in a (to her) entirely strange place and under (to her) definitely annoying circumstances, had asked her dinner for several days running, which suited her very well and was, for the Moritzes, a welcome change, because the Persian woman had, each evening, told them so much about her life, and in a manner that held their interest, and also included her life with the Swiss, that they were not bored for an instant, and he, Moritz, had actually tried, several times, to reach me, but I had been absolutely unreachable, locked in my house, into my *work prison*, as Moritz quoted me, I would not have let anyone into my work prison, I had never opened a window when he, Moritz, had knocked at the door, which was bound increasingly to confirm him in his belief that because of some, to him inexplicable, irritation I did not wish to have contact with him. I, as a person most receptive to such stories and accounts, and indeed hungry to receive them, as Moritz remarked about me, could not have enough of the stories and accounts of the Persian woman, who, he was certain of that, had become loquacious only after the Swiss had left. He, Moritz, had also incidentally mentioned my existence to the Persian woman and she had at once been very curious, but he had not told her any more about me than the most indispensable facts to satisfy her, that I was a friend of his, who ten or twelve years earlier, had, like herself, come to this region for the first time and bought from him a plot with a ruin standing on it and that I engaged in scientific studies. She absolutely had to meet me, he

101

had said to her, he was expecting me to turn up any day because, Moritz said about me, it was his friend's habit to drop in almost daily and spend the evening at his house. I did not come during periods of intensive work, Moritz had told her. I was probably, or certainly, in the middle of such a period now and for that reason did not drop in. He had made the Persian woman curious about me. But it had taken another three months before I made the Persian woman's acquaintance in the manner already outlined. I was now interested in discovering from Moritz as much as possible about the Swiss couple and especially about the Persian woman, about the time of her arrival and anything from the moment when they purchased their plot to the moment when I made their acquaintance, I had been so much impressed by my encounter with the Swiss couple the previous day that I could think of nothing else but to learn everything conceivable, even what might seem to him, Moritz, exceedingly trivial, about the Swiss couple. The Persian woman, I gradually learned from Moritz, came from a well-known family, quite definitely from the Iranian upper class, her early education had been first in Isfahan, then in England, and she had finally been sent to university in Paris. Her musical interest, as she had confided to Moritz at their very first meeting, had taken her to Vienna at the age of eighteen for several months, but she had not been there again since. The Swiss, who after his studies in Berne had himself attended a technical college in Paris, had, after a short acquaintance, entered into a closer and eventually a lasting relationship with her. One day the two of them had, against the wishes of their parents, moved in together and the Persian woman had, for the sake of her lover and his career, given up her own career, which meant that she had abandoned her philosophical studies for the sake of the Swiss. How far she had got in her studies I do not know to this day, but that is immaterial. She had only been nineteen and had, in the truest meaning of the word, surrendered herself and thenceforth devoted herself entirely to the professional advancement and promotion of her companion and lived entirely for the rise of the Swiss as an architect and eventually as a constructional engineer specializing in the building of power stations. Her own ambition for an absolutely and exclusively exceptional career for her life companion had taken root in her mind and her own existence had ultimately become totally subordinated to the existence of the Swiss. It is well known that women like the Persian woman are capable of giving up everything for the career of a men like the Swiss, and the Persian woman had in fact given up everything for her life companion, renouncing the development of her own astonishing gifts, probably overnight and in fact instantly. For the Asian female it is no more than natural that she subordinates and sacrifices herself to the male totally and in the most unreserved manner. That sacrifice ensures for her a *meaning to her life*. The two had come together at an ideal age for such a conjunction, she at nineteen, he ten years older, and had immediately assigned to themselves their lives' tasks by concentrating, right from the start, on developing the gifts of the Swiss as far as possible and to advance his career as far as possible. Such women as the Persian woman do not fail to notice the talent of a man that can be forced up to world fame, though he would never have achieved that by his own initiative. Men like the Swiss usually remain on the ground all their lives and achieve nothing more than a boring and uninteresting mediocrity unless they encounter women like the Persian woman. The Swiss had probably straight away perceived in the Persian woman the only chance in his life and made himself most readily available to the Persian woman's career ambitions, to what he may well have thought was an incredible experiment performed by her with his own gifts. His gifts and his mind had probably been ideally suited to her intentions and the

104

experiment had begun, immediately, while they were still in Paris. There may, because of all these career reasons, have existed between them an agreement that they would not marry, since marriage might, in certain circumstances, have wrecked their plan and it is possible that, at least initially, the intention, or perhaps even the vow, not to marry originated from her, that seems highly probable given the sophistication and the fine intellectual frame of the Persian woman. Thus, unmarried, they had jointly and at the same time independently concentrated on their task in life, on their true purposes in life, on far greater possibilities of development from the start. Moreover, the greatest stimulant of their alliance was the fundamentally different origin of the two, in terms of race and background. They must, at least during the initial period, have regarded one another as the ideal complement. As for the Swiss, Moritz reported that his father used to run a small shop in Zug, where, just as in our Austrian general stores, everything might be bought that was needed for everyday life, which reminded him, Moritz, that his own father had likewise owned a small shop and that Moritz himself had started out as a shop assistant and later as a small shopkeeper. He had come to so-called real-estate dealing rather late in life, not till his late fifties. From the city of Linz, the most repulsive and most thoroughly ugly Austrian town, which had been his home, he had intended to retire to the country and run a shop in the country, and for that purpose had bought property here in this neighbourhood. As, however, the purchase of his chosen plot of land had eaten up all his money he had been forced to sell off a small part of his property again, and to his enormous astonishment had received, for that small portion of his land, as much as he had originally paid for his whole property; in this way he had, almost unwittingly, discovered a taste for dealing in real estate and had immediately switched to that line of business. The Swiss is an illustration of a man coming from a modest, indeed an exceedingly modest (Zug) background, meeting, at the to him crucial, life-deciding moment, a person constructed with absolute precision just for him and his gifts, and then being, by this, to him in absolutely every respect crucial, person, guided upwards and led upwards to the greatest heights. The Swiss therefore was not one of those people whose great talent, just because it is not taken up and correctly taken hold of by such a life-deciding person as the Persian woman, is doomed to atrophy. If only we knew how many millions of extraordinary talents have to atrophy throughout the world every day just

106

because they are not taken up or taken hold of and developed, and eventually developed to the greatest heights! The Swiss was simply one of those people who, as regards their talent, are unable by nature to walk alone, in contrast to those who can only walk alone and can only develop their talents alone and develop them up to the greatest heights. He was one of those people who cannot on their own make anything of themselves and therefore cannot make anything of their talent or of their talents, because he was a weak person, in contrast to those strong people who can only develop their talents on their own, always entirely on their own, and develop them up to the greatest heights. In that respect the Swiss had been extremely fortunate to come across the Persian woman with her truly supreme willpower. However, she smoothed his path, and subsequently all paths, not only inwardly but outwardly. She had not only, from childhood on, always achieved whatever she had desired, but she also had always had access to the decisive social strata and therefore to the trendsetters and to the powerful. Once his, the Swiss's capabilities had been sufficiently developed, he had no need to worry about suitable large-scale commissions. But she did not give him anything for nothing, just as, eventually, he did not give himself anything for nothing, having thoroughly realized what was at stake. Their joint existence, from the moment they had their goal clearly before their eyes, that is the top rung of his career ladder, could only be an existence focused more and more on the ultimate limit of their capabilities and aimed at nothing else but that, for them suddenly exclusive, sole goal. From then on there was no room in them for anything else. Up to the moment when they arrived here they had lived together for just over four decades and during those four decades the Swiss had built four major power stations, that is one power station in each decade. I was reminded, as I was saying this to Moritz, of the photographs the Swiss had handed round when I first met him, which showed him shaking hands with the Queen of England, with the President of the United States, with the Shah of Persia and with the King of Spain. There is one photograph still missing, I had said to Moritz, showing the Swiss shaking hands with the President of Venezuela. One day, I joked, the Swiss will show us that photograph, with him, for the last time, shaking such an *exalted hand*. I had hoped the Persian woman would come to Moritz's in the evening but I waited in vain. Although the Swiss had again driven to Switzerland overnight, as I now learned from Moritz, the Persian woman had not come to

108

Moritz's house. Basically I was quite pleased, because I was hoping that when I next met her I would see her alone. I had let her know that I would call for her for a second walk in the larch-wood. But I had no longer had the courage and quite simply no longer the strength to do so that evening. I suspected that this would not have suited her either, I do not know why. I had said goodbye to Moritz in a few words and gone home through the wood. The outcome of my visit to Moritz was more than instructive, I had learned a lot about the Swiss. Half the night was gone and I was still turning over in my mind what Moritz had told me. While falling asleep I was thinking that in the Swiss couple I now, all of a sudden, had people in the neighbourhood with whom a more demanding, and not just an ordinary everyday and year-round and forever increasingly mind-dulling, contact was possible. I placed my highest hopes in my contact with the Persian woman. That was the end of October, the season when, by nature, I am always compelled to exist at the highest degree of difficulty. I had had no right to expect that this year, any more than in the past, I would be saved from my depressions, which intensified with the whole force of their causes mainly in the afternoons, and then to the limit of what I could stand, yet this year the Swiss couple had saved me from my depressions; in so many past years I had not been saved from these depressions, they persisted and they were effective all through nature's decline right into December. But it was possible that, just because these depressions had been so much more severe and merciless this year than in past years, and because I would quite certainly have been killed by this year's depressions, the Swiss couple had turned up. Of course that is an absurd idea. On the other hand, as I have come to know for certain in the course of my life, it is the absurd ideas which are the clearest ideas, and the most absurd ideas are the most important. I had thought that by withdrawing from my scientific studies and by once more remembering my great love of music and by engrossing myself in Schumann, from late summer onwards, I might escape my sickness, but this had proved an error. Music this year did not have the effect on my mind and on my whole being that it had had in past years, it had always been music which saved me from certain decline and from ruin, but this means of salvation did not work this year. I had, as I can again visualize myself clearly, summoned up all the strength at my disposal and taken the Schumann scores and gone to the coldest room in my house, the one next to my library, the one I called my *spider room*, and had endeavoured once more to study Schumann. All my life I had been concerned with Schumann as with no other composer, Schopenhauer the philosopher on the one hand, and Schumann the composer on the other, but all of a sudden I had found no access to Schumann's music and I had thought: suddenly you cannot find access even to Schumann's music to which you always found access, Schumann's music had always been my salvation just as *The World as Will and Idea* by Schopenhauer on the other hand, and I had to give up my attempt to save myself from my depression through Schumann. After all, I had the ability, which only few people have, to withdraw with a full score and to hear the music noted down in the score, I did not need any instruments, on the contrary, I heard the music more clearly, more purely, without orchestral instruments, hearing its architecture, with the aid of the full score and of course in the greatest possible extreme silence, was to me authentic. For that absolute pitch is an indispensable prerequisite. Neither Schopenhauer nor Schumann had achieved even a mitigation of my condition, that is a calming of my emotional and my mental state, which were both affected by my sickness with equal intensity. Emotionally and mentally I was always in the same state. For years I had been able to save myself with Schopenhauer, or if not with Schopenhauer then with Schumann, but now the two, much as I tried, failed to have any effect on me. Just as if everything within me were dead with regard to Schopenhauer and Schumann. To those two in particular my entire being had always been most receptive and responsive, now I had neither mind nor intellect for them. And this fact, of not being saved either by Schopenhauer or by Schumann, this terrible discovery that it was possible to be actually dead towards Schopenhauer and towards Schumann, in mind and ear, this first-time discovery of being *immune* to philosophy and also to music, had probably precipitated me into that state of really not-being-able-to-bear-it-any-longer of my being, my mind and my body, and I had rushed out of my house and through the wood to Moritz's. And in point of fact, as I now remember, I had, as soon as I came to Moritz, said to him: *neither Schopenhauer nor Schumann*, which quite possibly he had been unable to understand because I had been unable to explain myself any further. The fact that all of a sudden I had no access either to Schopenhauer or to Schumann, to whom I had always had access as long as I can remember, had thrown me into that murderous state of panic and, if I did not actually want to go crazy or insane, I had to get out of my house and go to Moritz. The momentary horror of that attack at least resulted in my being driven by that horror out of my own house and to Moritz's. *Neither Schopenhauer nor Schumann* I had said to Moritz as I sat down in my corner seat in his box-file room, to pounce on him with my insanity and no doubt wounding him in the most shameless manner. And then suddenly the Swiss couple had turned up and walked into Moritz's house and that had been the turning point and therefore also my salvation. Because they had come to Moritz and into the box-file room with their very real issue, their principal issue, that is the construction of their house, the Swiss couple had been able to save me in their fashion. As a result of my being ignored, together with my problem, not only, as was quite natural, by the Swiss couple but also at that moment by Moritz, and I now believe by all of them in a probably life-saving manner, they saved me, and in point of fact there occurred an immediate calming of my emotional and mental state. And because the Swiss couple knew nothing at all about my state, because they could not know anything about that state or even have an inkling of what their arrival at Moritz's had produced within me, not having known before, all the conditions had been ideal for my salvation. And on the day following my encounter with the Swiss couple I had once more been able to

113

approach Schopenhauer (and subsequently also Schumann), I had again been able to read *The World as Will and Idea*. The experiment of listening to Schumann in the spider room upstairs had once more been successful. But if the Swiss couple had not arrived, and more particularly arrived at that crucial moment, I would probably have gone crazy or insane and would quite certainly not have survived. If, as has been shown by this *method* for some time and has also been medically confirmed, these attacks continue to intensify, and there can be no doubt about that, if only from the logic of past attacks, then I shall not have many more attacks. In that respect my future is clear to me and there would be no point in being precipitate. The existence I lead, which of course has long been led only by my sickness, has entered its terminal phase. If only I can now and again have a chance of studying *The World as Will and Idea*, studying *The World as Will and Idea* for the rest of my life and entering the spider room for the rest of my life, I believe, with the philosopher Schopenhauer on the one hand and with the composer Schumann on the other, and, I am quite logically developing my thought, with the composer Schopenhauer and with the philosopher Schumann, because although Schopenhauer is really a philosopher he is also a composer, and Schumann the composer is really a philosopher. Years ago I began an essay in which I tried to demonstrate the composer in Schopenhauer and the philosopher in Schumann, and then I put it aside, but perhaps this is the moment to take up that essay again. Just because I am still unable to engage in my scientific studies, *on the antibodies in nature*, and because in future, if indeed I have anything like a future, it will be necessary to intensify my studies of the antibodies in nature even further if I do not wish to run the risk of having finally foundered in my lifelong studies, this was the time when I should not neglect my *anti-studies*, my musical and philosophical ones and the philosophical-musical ones and vice versa, and perhaps I shall still have some time when I am able to pursue all those studies. What has occurred during the past few weeks is suddenly becoming clear, and it becomes bearable because I am trying, by putting these notes on paper, to make it bearable, and these notes have no other purpose than to record in writing my encounter with the Swiss couple and more particularly with the Persian woman and thereby to find relief and thereby possibly to open up once more an approach to my studies. By putting these notes on paper I hope to achieve several purposes simultaneously, on the one hand to record my recollections of the Persian woman and to improve my condition, to prolong my life, which I may possibly, just by putting these notes on paper now, succeed in doing. My past attempts at putting these notes on paper had failed, had been bound to fail, because quite simply the moment for them had not yet arrived, because I still lacked the necessary distance. But now I am able to put these notes on paper, incomplete though they inevitably are. The Persian woman has gone her way. It was, like all ways, a *humanly possible* way. From the moment she met her life companion, the Swiss, if not before, she could not have expected a different way. I had to remain in the dark on what her way had really looked like before she arrived here with the Swiss. On this point I received no more information than she had herself given me and I have to resort to surmise. But even if I had learned more about her it would certainly not have changed my impression of her as a failed human being. An existence as a humanly possible sacrificial mechanism, I would say. And that it was certainly no coincidence that she came across the Swiss in Paris in order to sacrifice herself to him. For four decades she had existed by the side of that man, more or less happy, perhaps even happy during certain quickly passing work-obsessed periods, in order to work on her life's objective, the rise of her man, the Swiss, who had been destined for that fame thrust upon him by her. For her, the Persian woman, this had not been an endless way, her life had passed quickly, everything about her confirmed this to me. And she could tell herself that she had *co*-constructed the four power stations which he had constructed. And whenever he, the Swiss, had shaken those *exalted hands* she had stood behind him, the photographs proved it. And then one day, at some moment that suited nature, their whole system had collapsed and they had decided to put an end to that continuous obsession, their megalomania, and they had started to look for a so-called *retirement plot*, and they had purchased the water-logged meadow behind the cemetery and had begun to build a house. And with what building eagerness the Swiss had got down to that job: while his real architect's mind was still on the uncompleted Venezuelan power station the footings of his *retirement home* were being set in concrete and the materials he required for completing the construction had been bought. One or two more trips to South America, as he had said, and that was all. The Persian woman had observed everything in continual silence and totally without comment. Her increasing passivity had begun to be irritating. The ruthlessness with which the Swiss, with increasing frequency it seemed, was acting against the wishes of his woman friend, and more and more frequently downright distastefully against her wishes, had been shocking. I do not know if she ever voiced any wishes with regard to the house behind the cemetery and beyond the wood, but it is certain that the Swiss would not have met any of her wishes in the slightest degree. On my second walk with the Persian woman, which, like the first one, again led us to the larch-wood, I observed that deep resignation which befalls shipwrecked persons from a certain moment onwards and then for the rest of their lives. This time we had not just gone into the larchwood wordlessly and deeper and deeper into the uncanny darkness, but straight away into a discussion regarding the situation of the Persian woman. *She* had begun it, *not me*, and *she*, much as I had a few days earlier poured out my heart to Moritz in the most desperate of all conditions, had poured out her intellect and her heart, and she had done so no less violently and no less ruthlessly to me than I had a few days before to Moritz. Just as though the Persian woman had been in the same situation as I had a few days before. And just as I, a few days before, had behaved to Moritz in the manner mentioned (though no more than adumbrated) above, so she now behaved to me, mercilessly to me and to herself, now she had me as her victim just as, a few days before,

I had had Moritz as my victim. It was as if during that walk in the larch-wood the pent-up decades with her companion, who, as she believed, was then in Switzerland, had all of a sudden erupted and forced her to speak out. From no person had I, up to that moment, heard anything more horrible about life and the world than from her, no one until then had dared to uninhibit himself towards me in such a self-destructive manner, and throughout that time, during that revelation process triggered by her and set in motion by her ever more frankly and more ruthlessly, I had to think that only a few days earlier Moritz must have undergone what I was now undergoing, that he could not have kept his horror at myself free from loathing at such infamy, any more than I did now *vis-à-vis* the Persian woman. Only now, in the course of this shameless self-revelation of the Persian woman, did I shield myself behind the thought of having turned my inside out before Moritz just as the Persian woman was doing now before me. But such an ultimately totally helpless person, as I suddenly realized, naturally needed my sympathy to a far greater degree. She had been unable to calm down and repeatedly declared that her whole life had become pointless, that everything in her life had quite consciously been tending towards an ultimately pointless and useless existence. She had joined up with the Swiss in order to *snub* her existence and had quite consciously performed this act of self-destruction. By joining up with the Swiss *she* had joined up with a talent and had loved that talent and its development potential, but not the Swiss as a person, as an individual, as a character; by him she had always been repelled. And so long as she had been able to develop the *talent* of the Swiss, a few times she had also said *the genius*, all had gone well, her system had only broken down the moment when the talent or the genius of the Swiss were no longer capable of further development. That was now over two decades ago. From that moment onwards everything had become even more horrible for her. Her life companion, the Swiss, was now having his revenge on her *gamble*, these were her own words, and was building this house behind the cemetery and beyond the wood in order to get rid of her. Now that she had grown old and ugly, she was approaching sixty and he was approaching seventy, he was withdrawing from her, leaving her in the lurch. She suspected that he had turned his interest to a Venezuelan nurse and basically did not wish to have anything more to do with her, the Persian woman. He had finished with her, she had finished with him. She was expected to move into that inhuman house behind the cemetery and beyond the wood, a house designed *against her*, the most frightful house imaginable. All that was left to her now was to remain silent about everything and to remain, totally dulled, in pointless and useless contemplation, without any influence with regard to the future. The Swiss had executed his plan against her with a clearly visible and of course, to his woman friend, perceptible expression of his destructive intention against her. And he had bought the building plot because it had been ideally suited to his purpose of, as he had allegedly said to her face, punishing her the way she deserved for her lifelong experiment on him. It was the most hideous plot he had ever seen. He had bought it because he had realized that he would not find another more hideous. Now I had the explanation. Moritz and I had thought the Swiss was crazy to buy the water-logged meadow, but now he was not crazy at all, he knew exactly what he was doing in buying that water-logged meadow. Now I also had an explanation for the strange wordless behaviour of the Persian woman during my first encounter with her. I cannot repeat all the things she said to me in the larch-wood, where, at the climax of her emotional and intellectual discharge, she had sat down on a tree stump, actually withdrawn into her Persian lamb coat. She could have been some animal, sitting there on the tree stump and pouring her inside out and eventually only crying. Was this not my own condition which the Persian woman, sitting now on that tree stump, was enacting for me? I was more nauseated by the scene than I was moved and I encouraged the Persian woman to get up and go home, which meant going back to the inn. On the way back I had the impression that she had found relief and inevitably I compared her way back home through the larch-wood with my own way back home from Moritz a few days earlier. What I had then been unable to say because I had no chance of doing so, she now said as we were walking towards the village, not a hundred steps from the first house, beyond which the inn could now be seen: that I had saved her. For many months, perhaps for many years, she had not been able to talk to anyone the way she had just talked to me, which meant nothing more than that for months and for years she had not come across anybody to whom she could have unburdened herself completely and in the most shameless and ruthless manner. She believed she had to thank me for my behaviour during her emotional and intellectual outburst and then, all of a sudden, clearly wanted to be left alone. I had walked home in a shocked and simultaneously totally sobered-up condition. The very next day I had again called for her and again walked with her to the larch-wood. Then, owing to her successful emotional and intellectual discharge of all inhibitions the day before she was in a totally different state, in one which matched my own state following my excesses before Moritz a few days earlier. Now we were truly able in all tranquillity to conduct a conversation, more particularly a conversation about Schumann, with whom she was familiar, indeed, which greatly surprised me and made me happy, extremely familiar. She too loved Schumann, she too was able to read full scores and to hear music in the most perfect manner solely from studying the score. Thus the two of us, all of a sudden, had a subject which ideally suited our condition and in which, each of us reviving the other, time and again encouraging and inspiring the one and the other, we were able to stride out in our minds and hence in our thoughts. The oppressive elements had suddenly vanished and her state was calm and thought-stimulating. I myself had been in a very similar state to hers, equally liberated. What I had hoped for on my first encounter with her at Moritz's house now seemed to have come about, that I would have an ideal partner for my mind and mood amidst this invariably mind-hostile and mood-killing neighbourhood. Of course I had not forgotten what she had revealed of herself the day before, that which was the *sinister* element in a human being, but this did not bother me at that moment any more than it bothered her, as we were drawing each other's attention to ever new beauty and peculiarities and openness and honesty in Schumann's music. It was a truly *musical* walk. Unlike the following day, when we had a thoroughly *philosophical* walk, for which, naturally, *The World as Will and Idea* had been the stimulus. But I could just as well now describe our first walk as a *philosophical* one and the second as a *musical* one, philosophy is music, music is philosophy, and the other way round. It is pleasant to be with a person for whom one's own concepts are just as clear and defined as they are for oneself. In the Persian woman, all of a sudden, I had such a person, one who had turned up by good fortune, whom, like so much else that had been my salvation in recent years, I owed to Moritz, I thought. Not a single day passed without me calling for the Persian woman at her inn and taking a walk with her. The larch-wood had been the refuge of the two of us every one of those days towards evening. The Swiss had nearly always been in Switzerland, or if he was in Austria he had been busy with the building of his house. He had pursued his distancing from his life companion quite consistently.

124

After I had made contact with the Persian woman and had increasingly intensified that contact, having actually entered into an emotional and intellectual relationship with her, he had totally dropped the pretence of harmony between himself and her and, towards the end of November, had no longer returned to his companion after a visit to Switzerland. He had transferred to her a substantial, to me unknown, sum of money and after that ceased all communication. By then the Persian woman had definitively stopped counting on him. She had not found it possible to accustom herself to the rough and cold and inhospitable nature of this region. Probably she had not even tried. The people here had struck her the way they really are, malicious and ruinous to all strangers. At the inn, as the innkeeper's wife told me, she had always sat in the corner on her own, drinking tea, drawing her Persian lamb coat even more tightly around her, in a permanent fear of freezing to death. She had come to realize, as I had, that those walks to the larch-wood were no solution either, not for her and not for me. After a while we took those walks at ever longer intervals. In the end, gradually, because we were both self-centred, each in his own way, and had both been far too long reduced to our own company, our topics of conversations had also worn thin and

125

had eventually been exhausted. In December we had only been meeting once a week. I had suddenly begun to find it unbearable to have to look at her, time and again, in her black Persian lamb coat, I simply could no longer bear that black Persian lamb coat. Suddenly also I could no longer bear her voice, and she probably felt the same with regard to me. Incredible how rapidly the best relationship, if it is stressed beyond its capacity, wears thin and finally exhausts itself. When we did meet it was by then a meeting in mutual irritation. To belittle everything before us and reciprocally. For a long time we had not talked about Schumann or about Schopenhauer, no longer about music and no longer about philosophy, it was by then a dull, world-accusing, and eventually doubly destructive period of depression with us. We had decided not to see one another again, but when I thought of her staying alone at that inn, in a neighbourhood she did not know and which, by the nature of things, could only frighten or at least always only irritate her, and among people who, out of stupidity and crudity, rejected her, I went time and again to the inn to see her and encouraged her, mostly against my own sentiments, to come for a walk in the larch-wood. Suddenly that person had become a stranger to me, had become totally estranged from my mind

and from my emotions. Now her existence had
become an obstacle to me, I felt that I might
be able to work again, to become involved
once more *with the antibodies*, if she were not
present. Suddenly she was paralysing me and
I resisted contact with her. One day, when I
tried to call on her again at the inn, I was told
by the innkeeper's wife that she had left the
inn and moved into her life companion's not
even half-finished house behind the cemetery
and beyond the wood, she had been unable to
stand the inn any longer, as the innkeeper's
wife gave me to understand, and also for fin-
ancial reasons. She, the innkeeper's wife, was
glad the Persian woman had gone, she had
been troublesome to her for a very long time
and since, apart from tea, she had consumed
nothing, she, the innkeeper's wife, had not
made anything out of her. Even the cigarettes
which she had continually smoked had been
bought from the shop and not from her, and
she, the innkeeper's wife, had eventually hated
that *person*, as in the end she called the Persian
woman. It was incomprehensible to her, the
innkeeper's wife said, what business such
surely *inferior foreigners* as the Persian woman,
whose husband had *for good reasons* run out
on her, had in this neighbourhood. She, the
innkeeper's wife, had described the Persian
woman as *trash*, while crediting her life

127

companion with at least some sound common sense, she had not disliked him but it was surely a mystery how such a *decent and educated man* could have picked up such a *worthless person* as the Persian woman. Only such a decadent person as myself, the innkeeper's wife remarked with her native frankness, could have taken up with a person like the Persian woman. Once again the innkeeper's wife described the Persian woman as *daylight-shy and work-shy trash* before I left the inn in order to call on the Persian woman at her home. This is what I found: half-way between the wood and the Persian woman's house a white ambulance came driving in the opposite direction and I immediately thought that in that ambulance with its red cross in front the Persian woman was being taken to hospital. I had stopped in alarm as the ambulance passed me, but on closer inspection I realized that while that ambulance had in fact once been an ambulance it had, as I assumed, been converted by Moritz into an ordinary van serving the transport of cement; inside the vehicle there had been two workmen who, in a drunken state, as I instantly observed, had evidently steered the vehicle through the loose stones and across the swampy ground in the wood. I had recognized the workmen as two of the ethnic Germans whom Moritz hired for his building purposes and presumably had put at the Persian woman's disposal for the continuation of the work on her house. My fears that something might have happened to the Persian woman were not confirmed. The house, as I immediately saw, was in an indescribably catastrophical condition, half-finished and already neglected and open to decay, it stood, already overgrown by luxuriant tall weeds, in the middle of the swamp and an evil smell had spread all around it. All the window shutters were closed and when I knocked at the door there was no reply. But I had reason to assume that the Persian woman was at home and I repeatedly knocked at the door, and kept knocking at the door until I heard sounds inside the house. From the house there was a view only in one direction and even that was virtually no view at all. It was three-quarters enclosed by the wood. The walls were blackened with damp and the footings had not even been entirely filled in yet. It looked as if the builders had abruptly stopped work, a lot of tools were still lying around in the mud. After a prolonged period of waiting the Persian woman eventually opened to me. I had of course come entirely unexpected and she had had no idea that it was me knocking at the door. She had thought that the ethnic Germans who had driven away in the converted ambulance had left something behind. I squeezed through the gap in the doorway and, after she had relocked the door, followed her to her room. Room, however, is certainly not the right word for the space to which she had retired. This was evidently the smallest room in the whole house, on the ground floor and utterly unsuitable as a room to live in; there were a few mattresses lying on the floor, covered with a sheet. In spite of the gloom, or almost darkness in the room, I was struck by the dirtiness of that sheet. When we had stepped into the room, in which there was a frightfully stale smell and dankness, the Persian woman, now wrapped in a long flannel dressing gown on which dirt and floral pattern were no longer distinguishable, lay down on the mattress and invited me to sit down on a chair which stood by the only window in the room. As I sat down I noticed how shabby and neglected and actually how deliberately grubby everything was in that room. Because of the darkness in the room I could not see the Persian woman's face, but on the way in I had had the impression that she had lost weight and gone grey. By her bed, at the head end, the Persian woman had two small tables piled high with nothing but medicines, as I believe exclusively sleeping pills. She had now been in that room for two weeks, she told me while my eyes were focused on those packets of medications and on her still not unpacked suitcases, and for those two weeks she had not left her house. Nor did she intend ever to leave it again. She did not eat anything, she only drank tea, and she wished for nothing except sleep. By taking ever stronger sleeping draughts and in ever greater quantities she actually still managed to sleep. If she woke it was only for the purpose of taking more sleeping pills. She had covered her uncurtained window with a whitish-grey American cloth, I noticed, and probably not opened it during those two weeks. She possessed a large tin of tea, still half-full, that was enough for her. She had been unable to stand the people at the inn. The company had disgusted her. For an instant, but that instant was now long gone, she had thought of returning to her home, to Persia. Or to Greece, where she had friends, but she had dropped the idea again. From me she had expected salvation, but I too had disappointed her. I was, much as she was, a lost and ultimately ruinous person, even though I did not admit that to her, she could feel it, she knew it. No salvation could come from such a person. On the contrary, such a person only pushed one even deeper into despair and hopelessness. *Schumann, Schopenhauer*, these were the two words she said after a prolonged silence and I had the impression that she was smiling as she said them, and then nothing again for a long time. She had had everything, heard and seen everything, that was enough. She did not wish to hear from anyone any more. People were utterly distasteful to her, the whole of human society had profoundly disappointed her and abandoned her in her disappointment. There would have been no point in saying anything, and so I just listened and said nothing. I had, she said, on our second walk in the larch-wood, been the first person to explain to her the concept of anarchy in such a clear and decisive manner. *Anarchy* she said and no more, after that she was again silent. An anarchist, I had said to her in the larch-wood, was only a person who practised anarchy, she now reminded me. *Everything in an intellectual mind is anarchy*, she said, repeating another of my quotations. Society, no matter what society, must always be turned upside down and abolished, she said, and what she said were again my words. Everything that is is a lot more terrible and horrible than described by you, she said. You were right, she said, these people here are malicious and violent and this country is a dangerous and an inhuman country. You are lost, she said, just as I am lost. You may escape to wherever you choose. Your science is an absurd science, as is every science. Can you

132

hear yourself? she asked. All these things you yourself said. *Schumann and Schopenhauer*, they no longer give you anything, you have got to admit it. Whatever you have done in your life, which you are always so fond of describing as *existence*, you have, naturally enough, failed. You are an absurd person. I listened to her for a while, then I could bear it no longer and took my leave. When I was outside, in the middle of the wood, I once more said to myself aloud the last of her sentences: do not visit me again, leave me alone. I have, against all opposition within me, stuck to that sentence. I never visited her again. For a long time I heard nothing more from her. Early in February, to be exact on the seventeenth, the day after my birthday, I came across an utterly strange item in the newspaper, one which immediately touched me: a foreign woman, her origin not specified, had thrown herself under a lorry loaded with several tons of cement near Perg in the Mühl-viertel, possibly with suicidal intent. At once I thought of the Persian woman. It seemed the obvious thing for me to go and see Moritz to find out if there was anything in my surmise. Moritz had already been informed of the accident, but he knew no details. Ten or eleven or twelve days afterwards he had discovered the following: the Persian woman had pulled on her Persian lamb coat one day and had gone through the wood right into the village and then taken a train to Perg. What she wanted there is unknown. In Perg, having got off the train, Moritz said, she had sat down in the station buffet and drunk a glass of hot tea. She had paid and had got up and straight out of the buffet had walked into a lorry passing at that moment with a load of several tons of cement. Her corpse had been dreadfully mutilated. Moritz had found out that, since no one knew where she came from or who she was, she had been buried in a common grave at the Linz cemetery fourteen days after the accident. He, Moritz, had been unable, *a mere fourteen days after her burial*, to discover from the cemetery administration in which common grave. He had then, having been able to inform the authorities of the identity of the deceased, notified her life companion, the Swiss, of the tragedy. The Swiss, however, had not reacted at all. As I left Moritz's house I saw the Persian woman's black Persian lamb coat hanging in the Moritz vestibule next to his own mouse-grey winter overcoat. The authorities had handed the coat over to him. As well as her handbag. Two days later, when I walked over to the totally abandoned, not yet half-finished and already dilapidated, house in the water-logged meadow, it occurred to me that on one of our walks in the larch-wood I had said to the Persian woman that so many young people nowadays killed themselves, and that the society in which those young people were compelled to exist was totally unable to understand why, and that, quite out of the blue and in fact in my tactless way, I had asked the Persian woman if she would kill herself one day. Upon which she had only laughed and said *Yes*.